# NOT BY BREAD ALONE

# NOT BY BREAD ALONE

a novel by

Naomi Mitchison

Marion Boyars
London · New York

Published in Great Britain and the United States in 1983 by
Marion Boyars Ltd.,
18 Brewer Street, London W1R 4AS
and by
Marion Boyars Inc.,
457 Broome Street, New York, NY 10013.
Distributed in The United States by
The Scribner Book Companies, Inc.

Australian and New Zealand distribution by
Thomas C. Lothian Pty.,
4-12 Tattersalls Lane, Melbourne, Victoria 3000.

**British Library Cataloguing in Publication Data**
Mitchison, Naomi
  Not by bread alone.
  I. Title
  823'.912[F]        PR6025.I86
  ISBN 0-7145-2788-2 Cloth

**Library of Congress Cataloguing in Publication Data**
Mitchison, Naomi, 1897–
  Not be bread alone.
  I. Title.
PR6025.I86N6   1983      823'.912      82-17738

For Graeme
and his dragons

# FOREWORD

The action of this book starts perhaps some twenty years
from now and goes on for another generation or so. During
that time I have assumed the formation of an autonomous
Aboriginal State in Northern Australia, extending eastward
along the northern coast to include some of what is now
Queensland territory. It is called Murngin, somewhat
accidentally, after one of many kinship groups or hordes
(much as England was accidentally called after the tribe of
Angles or as many a lake or mountain after long-forgotten
officials or royalties). I assume that Darwin will be the capital
of a predominantly white State of Northern Australia.

All names, organizations and characters in this novel are
fictitious and any resemblance is purely accidental.

# CHAPTER ONE

It had all begun years ago when they were both in some ways different people. Yes, it began with the first probings into the hidden complications in the layers of normal leaf structure. There were thoughts, at first random but then structured, on what might happen if a shift of cells could be induced to succeed. Over the months there had been the hunt through any relevant papers, not always in the obvious journals and a long discussion between them as to what might be involved. That developed into watching and testing, more than three years' work from the beginning, and the sudden realization that what was actually coming up was far more exciting and important than anything which had earlier seemed likely or even possible.

'Well, we seem to have gone through all the possible checks we can think of,' Anne Tomlin said, frowning a little. Her hands were clenched tight inside the pockets of her lab coat. She shook her head, half unwilling to believe what they had both been trying to actualize, to put into unmistakable words and figures.

'So this seems to be, well, my dear Anne, the proof of what did not seem possible.' His voice went up and down answering her. Saranjit Singh wore the same kind of white lab coat, but it looked different on him because of his netted beard and turban. Similar visualizations and ideas were going through both their minds. There were the measurements, above all of the startling jumps immediately after the chloroplast re-arrangement. There were the repeats in all the necessary differences of environment and temperature; it had all taken what seemed an intolerable length of time, years of work, but that was the price of certainty. And there pinned up on the wall were the micro-photographs of those elegantly dislocated leaf layers which in turn had set off the changes in the plant pattern, above all the effect of the suddenly increased supplies from leaf to ovule.

Yet, all the same, neither of them looked at what was inside the damp-clouded bell jars. Nor did those rather ordinary-seeming, large green leaves seem anything worth a second glance. Not, that is, unless the observer happened to be a botanist and had read and understood the Latin names on the labels, and had realized that these names referred to something quite other in the plant world, something small and unimportant. Not these. Yes, they were very odd plants, the closer you looked at them. It was not only their size, but their morphological relationships seemed to have gone askew. For example the gross seed-heads which should have been insignificant, were out of all proportion with the stems and leaves.

'If, even now,' she said, 'there was something we had left out or not reckoned with – I feel – Saranjit, it doesn't seem quite real.'

'You are thinking, Anne, that because we had begun to wish so much for our concept and its results to be proved fact, part of the material world, we did not perceive some flaw in our thinking – in our methods perhaps? Is that it?'

'No, not that. But – if this manipulation could be repeated

in other plant forms; in the cereals, as we have both thought –' He nodded. 'Well then, it would – it might – make the kind of difference which we cannot, now, foresee.'

'You mean,' he said, 'a social difference. I too have thought.'

'It might be for good, Saranjit,' she said with a choke of moral embarrassment.

'That won't be for us to decide,' he said, 'any more than Rutherford decided what was to be done with his split atom. . If he had known ... But I cannot think that what we have succeeded in doing can ever be hurtful.'

'Perhaps not,' she said. 'But it could make – a difference. You never know.' She shivered. It was the air conditioning. She had never liked it. But without it the afternoon heat tended to send one to sleep and that was a stupidity. 'I can't see, myself, how it could be used for – war for instance. No. It ought to be good. It ought to be developed.' She looked across at him: did she see doubt? 'Well,' she said in a different voice, 'whether we like it or not, we'd better start writing it up.'

'Yes, indeed,' he said, and then 'Funny, isn't it, that plants have so little – how shall I say – scientific honour – compared with animals, or rather, perhaps, animal matter. Even botany, poor little word, has a greyish connotation.'

'Instead of greenish!' she said and they both giggled. Being colleagues meant that quite stupid jokes were part of a much more subtle communication. They had been working together so long and, latterly, so tensely, that now a kind of childish relief was in order. 'I really must escape from your air conditioning!' said Anne Tomlin, and now her head was high and her tight fists unclenched: 'Now we can sit on the verandah.'

9

'It is still hot' said Saranjit Singh, but he followed her out into the warm evening. They had walked through the new laboratory building into the old house and through the high-ceilinged hall with the curious formal portrait of Anne's grandfather by an Indian artist. The verandah was amply wide; in full mosquito time it could be screened, but the season was not yet. One of the older servants brought them fresh lime, nimbupani in ice-cold tumblers; watching them refreshed his smile was gentle, as his bare feet were gentle on the matting. He remembered Anne's grandfather, to whom the bungalow had once belonged, ah, away back, before the laboratory buildings and the new office and the shining glass.

Anne, too, remembered the old look of things. But care had been taken not to damage the great garden. Here in the long curves of the shaded beds, past the lily pond and the green-stained lion fountain, there flourished in early Spring the high summer annuals of England, dwarf phlox, zinnias, carnations and Indian pinks, marigolds, asters and stocks, and mignonette with autumn backing them in hollyhocks and massed dahlias. But in another month all would be finished, dried into dust. Yet the best of the flowers were Asian or Polynesian, hibiscus and bougainvilleas in a hundred colours, the creepers that the sun-birds loved, the climbing cactus and the orchids, or the twisted buds of the moonflowers opening into sudden, quivering whiteness. At the back were old trees, towering dark-leaved figs, forever making their branch caves, or half-wild mangoes fluttering with fruit bats in the ripening months. There were guavas and loquats, fruiting palms and the glow of citrus fruits. But among them a few splendid flowering trees shone with gold and red or dropped their carpets, scented for a day, then rotting into soil.

But was it possible, Anne thought, that some day, in the future, there would be new plants, yes, plants designed and worked on by people, here, even here in her grandfather's garden?

She looked round. Was Saranjit thinking of that too? Or was he wanting to go back to his own house, to Nandu and the children? No, probably not. Not quite yet. So they sat watching the quick dusk fall, the stars blinking out, aware of the strengthening flower scents, two distinguished scientists, although in the unfashionable side line of plant morphology. And through and alongside their awareness of the natural world was the question of what – perhaps – would come of the work they had been doing, thinking all the time only in terms of the next step, not of its further consequences.

# CHAPTER TWO

The Chairman looked round his board room, gathering attention.

'This may be a nonsense, that is to say, from our own and our shareholders' point of view. But if it is a genuine possibility, I am sure you will all agree that we must make further enquiries without waiting. If necessary we must act on them. It would be a disaster if this were to fall into less, shall I say, scrupulous hands.' Yes, they were attending, giving the signs he knew fairly well, the hands flicking non-existent dust, the twitch of shoulders, the eyes fixing. It wasn't the whole Board, of course; that wouldn't have done. But the ones that mattered, yes.

He went on, 'From the point of view, not only of PAX, but also of, well, the civilized world – our own world – something of this importance should not be allowed to go where it might be wrongly used. There are those, I hardly have to remind you, even in top positions, who cannot be trusted to keep their mouths shut.'

It was a long time since Sir Edmund – but he had only been plain Ed Green in those days – had taken Biology 'A' levels. His life had followed a different path since then, in fact several paths. But at least he had more idea of what plant morphology was about than most of the others, although several knew more than you might think and ex-Professor Ferguson who had once been a physicist of no great originality before he went into Administration, still had a shrewd eye on what might be happening in the scientific world. He had some valuable contacts and some fore-knowledge of what the Chairman was going to say.

Sir Edmund went on:

'Plants. Think of plants and you think of flowers. Or tree trunks. But that isn't what matters. Basically, plants are leaves, circles and spirals of leaves. They grow this way; they have to, couldn't manage otherwise. Those trunks, they're there to hold up the leaves. Those flowers, they're leaves that have taken on another job. Ever cut a bud across? Well, I think you should. The leaves are doing this immensely com-plicated job of keeping the plant going, working in with the roots. We've all heard of chlorophyll, but those funny little cells that make leaves green are doing something far more complex than anyone suspected in the old days, not just the old oxygen-carbon dioxide exchange, but sifting in and out minute quantities of this and that, dealing with temperature and moisture. And other leaf cells – did you know that any leaf is made up of a whole series of layers interacting with one another? I could draw you a diagram – '

He looked as if he was going to, but Ferguson said sharply 'Let's get to the point, Edmund.'

Sir Edmund continued:

'Well: if you can make changes in the leaf layers, these influence the whole plant. There are things called auxins – but I won't go into that now. It's comparatively unimportant compared with the real breakthrough. The new input can make a vast difference to other parts of the plant, including the ovule. And the ovule, let me remind you, is what turns into the seed: wheat, rice, maize, barley, millet, sorghum.'

'The food grains' said Madame Raffray, almost to herself, 'the staff of life.'

'Exactly' said Sir Edmund, 'not to speak of beans, nuts, fruits and such. So that modifications of the internal structure of the leaf, what is called morphogenesis, can affect the crop – unbelievably.'

Another voice: 'And – perhaps other parts of the plant – the petals, you said?'

'Yes, Alberto. Not perhaps so importantly, but – yes, I understand some of the experimental work was done on flowers, though not so far on any kind which are commercially important. But certainly that could happen. One day, Alberto, that carnation you always wear could be – twice the size.'

Alberto gave a little lip twist, as though not relishing the idea, and Ruiz the Mexican threw himself back in his chair: 'Big carnations! What are you really after, Ed?'

13

Sir Edmund looked at him with a small smile: 'Something else comes in. You remember N.I.F.? Nitrogen fixing? That's one.'

Madame Raffray – and what was her pre-marital nationality? what was that delicate accent? – asked. 'But surely, Sir Edmund, we have already some involvement there?'

'Yes, indeed,' he answered, 'and the fact that we are, in a manner of speaking involved, will have considerable importance. The transfer of *rhizobium* bacteria – you recollect? Naturally, we have been in touch with the International Centre in Colombia.'

'And F.A.O.' said Ferguson, frowning a little, 'got to be correct. What about *azolla*?'

'Naturally we have been watching. But useless for dry-land crops, as you know.' He nodded. 'Well, we have achieved the transfer of *rhyzobium* bacteria from leguminous plants to some type of cereal – a lasting transfer, let me say. This has taken place in two experimental farms attached to the laboratories which, I am proud to say, we funded.'

'So that's where all the money went!' Ruiz the Mexican said. 'Devilish dear.'

'I recollect you were against it,' Sir Edmund said smoothly, 'but now we shall see the results.' Looking past Ruiz he noticed that two or three of the others were whispering and taking notes; yes, very properly. He went on. 'There are certain other transfers which appear to be in an advanced state. This has not yet been made public.'

'These scientists,' said Gustavsen, the heavy Swede, 'they will want to publish. Always the same. To get their names in print.'

'A very laudable desire to spread scientific knowledge,'

14

said Sir Edmund, 'but fortunately we can, I hope, arrange, so to speak, for a marriage.

'As a result, the same plants which, we hope, will carry the vastly improved cereal ovules – indeed whatever ovules can be improved in any plant form – will also carry rootlets which can achieve nitrogen fixation, thus cutting out a vast element of fertilizer expense.'

'Phosphates however – ' That was the American, Dr. Schulman, a darkish, short-haired little lady in large horn-rims.

'There are certain ideas about that, still, if I may so phrase it, in embryo. There is also the work on partially desalinated water usages. A countryman of yours, Professor Ferguson.'

'Aye, well, Ritchie; but it was only his grandparents went out from Oban.'

'To the drier climate of South Australia. Just so. That project has progressed in certain ways and we have been able to – well, to be in a position to use results in a relatively rapid manner. But I am anxious that the basic work on plant morphology should be placed firmly under the PAX mantle. It would then be exploited in the completely ethical manner in which PAX, I am proud to say, has always operated.' He looked around; several nodded solemn agreement. 'Thus these, so to speak, marriages can be arranged under our – controlled auspices.'

'Our blessing' said Madame Raffray, 'and hope of offspring. You tell us, Sir Edmund, that these so strange, so exciting leaf changes have in fact been, experimentally at least, achieved?'

'There are still problems. For example, in certain modified leaf forms, size is affected by hairiness, a matter of increasing area to meet volume. You follow me?'

15

'All sounds a trifle unlikely.' Ruiz again, his voice grating.

'I know. However, it seems – ' he looked at the typescript again, and shook his head almost imperceptibily – and yet, and yet. 'If, as I said, my friends, this is credible, there have been really extraordinary displacements of living plant tissue whose functions are in some way excited – I am not really competent to say how – so that not only is the actual leaf area vastly enlarged but corresponding quantities of the plants' needs are pumped in. There are plenty of puzzles not really solved, for example the spring rise of sap – yes, Alberto, Virgil knew it, but didn't know how it was done! How proteins are made. A whole chemical factory in those pretty leaves. But these people seem to have found out what's at the bottom of it.'

'Increased protein?' asked Dr. Schulman, 'to the ovule?' Sir Edmund nodded, and passed a xerox down to her. Several board members took one, including, he noted, Madame Raffray. What could she make of it?

'You tell us that this in real fact has been done?' Ruiz leaned forward, clearly disbelieving.

'Apparently. This copy that I hold has been taken from a learned journal of some distinction. And, to most business people, obscurity.' They took his point. 'One author is Saranjit Singh – '

'An Indian, a Hindu, they make up these things. Well do I know them!' That was Gustavsen. Old Lady Martin frowned, seemed about to speak, but as usual, thought better of it. Arrogant man! Still stuck with Gustavus Adolphus and the nasty European past, but let us hope the Chairman –

Yes, Sir Edmund is correcting him. 'A Sikh. I understand most reputable. Not merely in India. Has published in *Nature* and *Science*, as well as in journals which you and I would

16

find more obscure. The other author is Anne Tomlin. She is also highly reputable, would probably have been made a Fellow of the Royal Society if she had stayed nearer London. However, she has long-standing family connections with the East, though doubtless the main reason for the work being done out there is the rapidity of growth and generation. Some of the early work on this subject was done in India, as a matter of fact.'

'Doing your homework' said Ferguson with approval, and added: 'A tropical climate would halve the time for this type of experiment.' He had looked at the summary of the paper. Would read and digest later.

Sir Edmund looked around slowly. Several of the Board were frowning, making notes, whispering to one another. But, on the whole, he thought, approving. That big Swede would take some convincing, but it might be necessary, the Chairman thought, to arrange a visit to the Research Station where this was all going on. And to do it soon. Several of the board members knew enough science to be able to evaluate what was happening on the spot. Dr Schulman was asking: 'This is nothing to do with, let's say, polyploids?'

'No, no, it is far bigger. Different in kind. We don't begin to know if these ... alterations can be inherited. Probably not. They would have to be reproduced in some other way.'

'Cloning' said Ferguson. He had thought about it.

'The main thing is to get our hands on them. Now. I can foresee new plants being devised, custom-built, so to speak –'

'Dreams, my dear Edmund' said Alberto.

'No. This is real. And it is within our reach, though it may not be for much longer.' he tapped the paper. It was essential to convince them: quickly. The best way would be to take some of them over. Perhaps one of the ladies. Anne Tomlin

17

might talk more easily. Madame Raffray for instance. Madame? Was she ever, as a matter of interest, married? Knows a lot more than you might think, looking at her. And looking at her clothes. And her jewellery. Yes, she appeared to be reading the Xerox with – could it be? – understanding. We could get out there in a day, he thought, looking round, catching glances, all as easy as a bus ride except the last bit. But we'd better make it snappy in case someone else –. Now had he got them firmly onto the right track? 'You all see the possibilities?' he asked.

'Yes,' said the Mexican, 'they are considerable. Even in the political field. Especially in that field.' Stupid man, thought Madame Raffray, still with one foot in that old ruling European past, Spain! But let it pass; she made a little moué at Lady Martin, who had also noticed. Men! He scratched his head. 'But what about profits?'

'They will appear, I believe,' said Sir Edmund, 'satisfactorily. That is, if we succeed in persuading this group to accept our help.'

Ruiz nodded. 'I see. Up to us to get hold of these people. Who else can have seen the paper?'

'We cannot be sure. But the language is highly technical. I was fortunate that it was pointed out to me. By – well, a friend. However, we are making enquiries.' Discreet enquiries.

'I am making the supposition,' said Ferguson, 'that if this works out as you say, on a given acreage of land the crop could be, say, five times as large?'

'That would be an under-estimate' said Sir Edmund. For a minute nobody said anything.

Then it was Alberto. 'So, if this works out – if – as you said, Ed, if it is not a nonsense, then we could feed the world.'

Sir Edmund agreed. The Swede suddenly came to life.

18

'Which should be grateful to us! Which shall be!'

'And show it,' said Ruiz, 'and show it!' Lady Martin frowned. These men!

Madame Raffray had a question. 'Let us think in a practical way about these new food plants. Presumably they would have to be reproduced in some way; I think, Professor Ferguson, you mentioned cloning. So that there would be thousands – millions – of tiny rice or wheat plants, all with this vast improvement. Beautiful. But even with the NIF genetic input, would they require correspondingly large amounts of other fertilizers? That, if you recall, was where the green revolution ran into difficulties.'

'Not necessarily,' said Sir Edumund, 'the future is open. I can visualize plants being programmed to get all their needs from air and water. Perhaps even P and K. Simply. Even from undrinkable water, of which there is an almost indefinite amount on this planet. Or again, plants could be programmed to grow in hitherto impossibly arid or heavily frosted areas. Yes, using the whole of the Earth! But there would have to be, necessarily, several years of trials. However, it is quite possible that PAX funding would help considerably with this, as it has done with nitrogen fixing and to a lesser extent with the saline water problems. Scientists often have excellent ideas and not sufficient practical help in carrying them out. We shall have to see whether the present centre could be enlarged.'

'We might,' said Madame Raffray, 'have to persuade the scientists that enlargement would be sensible.'

'In their interest' said Alberto.

'I feel sure that our practical help, in one form or another, will be appreciated,' said the Chairman, 'bringing this experimental work into genuine and beneficial fruition.'

19

'And the Garden of Eden' said Madame Raffray, 'in which Adam and Eve wanted nothing except dress.'

'Which also we might be able to provide.' The Chairman smiled at her. A helpful and above all attractive woman, but yet – always a little remote. There were occasional rumours about her past life; it was said that she had been a dancer and after that had gone through a period of intense education. Which might be all nonsense. And Raffray – what had he been? Had he, indeed, existed? And where had the money, the undoubted money, come from? One took her out to lunch and it was all very pleasant, but, somehow, nothing changed, no new light. He went on: 'I can visualize our cottons knocking out all the artificials. They would be designed for split-minute machine picking, naturally. And the health angle; no irritations, no allergies, pure vegetable fibre! However, Madame, I am afraid this is still some way off. Not that we need not think ahead. Imagine ahead even. But at this stage I must remind you all that it merely seems – yet what a big merely! – that the growth patterns of some plants at least can be controlled artificially: given sufficiently informed programming. Which has yet to be worked out on the basic industrial crops, we trust with help from ourselves. So it is all a few years on.'

'And hunger is still there,' said Madame Raffray, looking critically at her finger nails, 'hunger and hatred. But if everybody had all they needed – '

'Food for the world,' said Sir Edmund.

'Yes, but – ' Ruiz began. Only then they all started talking at once, while a thought went through Madame Raffray's head: Not by bread alone, yes, but without bread – and then there was a gentle cough from Lady Martin. 'I think,' she said, 'that we must all by now realize that Food Aid has not necessarily helped the hungry. Either it has not got to them owing to local corruption or politics, or else it has discouraged them from making efforts to feed themselves. Have we considered this? Have you, Sir Edmund?'

'Indeed I have,' he said. 'Naturally. A detailed memorandum will be placed before the Board. And, at the very best, it will be some years before – well, before we see our first field of the new wheat.' He stopped for a moment, gathering looks. 'But I envisage food being grown as nearly as possible on the spot under our direct supervision, employing the same people and of the same kind that those people are used to and want.'

Lady Martin relaxed a little. But there was some alarm among other board members. The Chairman, as usual, running ahead of them. Envisaging! On the strength of one paper in a scientific journal! But perhaps that was why he was Chairman.

Professor Ferguson remarked 'indeed, yes. We shall need to be in control. From the beginning. Let us hope that the authors of this paper can be induced to realize the – probabilities.'

'The moral burden upon them and ourselves,' said Lady Martin softly. She was looking into the future. Alberto, who liked her very much but never managed to say so and never would, nodded agreement. Yes, we must be serious. Not only for ourselves.

Not only for ourselves? For a short time the Chairman had been thinking simply in terms of the Board. Whom he liked on the whole and even to some extent admired. But who were not quite so important as some of them liked to think. For of course there was the Corporation and it was important to keep a clear distinction, for himself at any rate. A simple little matter of arithmetic. Feeding the world would cost a considerable amount – let us not lose ourselves in the millions – sums which appear almost impossibly large to most people, so that they totally fail to take them in. But set that against the profits which the Corporation in all its branches is going to make in supplying what the no longer hungry people will want next – ah, then! He doubted whether all the PAX Board recognized the existence of the Corporation, although no doubt they did know that the Board was involved with other interests. He looked benevolently round the table, Dr Schulman, Alberto perhaps, Ferguson, Lady Martin, Madame Raffray. But here he hesitated. Yes, it seemed highly probable that she did know.

# CHAPTER THREE

Marie-Claire Raffray looked with very great care at the memos from the board secretariat. There was always a faint inhuman smell when they first slid out of the teleprinter into her hand. Were others aware of it as she was? She had once asked Dr Schulman – surely another woman might have noticed it. But not the Schulman; perhaps Americans have less sense of smell. You might guess this from their perfumes. Perhaps they have also less awareness of the exact import of an apparently straightforward statement.

There was one of the secretariat in particular whom she

could trust – and she smiled a little – a fan, as in the old days. Before she changed her name. Had she changed anything else? She flexed and extended her right leg, tried out the foot muscles and looked at it critically. Yes, it would do. One or two items in the memoranda had the erased M at some point which meant that they should be followed up.

And the Chairman should at the next meeting understand that they had been followed up, if not by everyone at least by her. A curious fellow the Chairman, both tough and flexible, looking a long way. Sometimes further than she did herself but not every time. He had made a bad mistake in his first approach to the scientists: oh that letter! Just as well that he had asked her – and of course the others – to go later. Otherwise, yes, otherwise ... Nor was Edmund's knowledge of science as deep as he would like the rest, especially Professor Ferguson, to suppose. And on this present necessary aspect he had not had the teaching from scientists which she herself had taken in. Ah, the teaching! Nor had he seen these astonishing products. Yes, he had seen them certainly in close-up video but not with his total senses alerted, as hers had been.

That first day with Anne Tomlin. How had Anne realized that it was so necessary to teach her, or rather perhaps that she was the one whom it was so necessary to teach? Or was that how it had been? Anne teasing a little, and did she always tease? Something to find out. Later. So whose doing was it? One never knew. Nor would she herself remember the relevant facts of morphogenesis in the same way that the Chairman probably does: cerebrally. But am I certain of that? I very much doubt if any of us are completely certain about our dear Edmund. Has he a private life? Who knows? Perhaps someone on the secretariat? Like my little lady. Or probably not. She giggled quietly to herself, went back to the figures.

She lived in a Manoir in the Burgundy valley – where else could one live? Yes, at certain seasons back in Mauritius, but she had a dislike of cyclones, so disrupting of thought or indeed anything else, including communication. Her little Burgundian airstrip was so handy, scarcely more than a ten minute flight to Dijon. Video reception was perfect. There was a mirrored room where she still practised at the bar and her garden, the shades and lights of it, the sparkle of water. Some day perhaps with Anne – strange to begin dreaming again.

And it had all started with her own willingness to learn, to learn completely, not simply to have some finished effect demonstrated to her. She had the basics of biology and indeed agriculture. Had she not been successful in the introduction of a new variety of cane on her uncle's Mauritius estate? – but of course they had dropped it after a couple of seasons in spite of the good results. Laziness! She herself was not lazy. 'Anne,' she had said, 'may I perhaps call you Anne? There are certain processes I have not completely grasped. Is it too much to ask you to demonstrate again?' And it was not too much. Ferguson had dropped out, claiming that now he had everything clear in his mind. Perhaps he thought he had understood it all, though this was doubtful. He had been feeling the heat when they were outside. Also he thought their mission had been completely successful and would so report. The Board's first grants to the Centre – no strings! – had borne ample fruit. Now was the moment for the big move.

But had Anne Tomlin been completely persuaded? It is difficult sometimes for a scientist to grasp totally the possibilities in a world of politics and these other aspects of reality. Yes, Anne was deeply interested in the scientific possibility for further work, with no pecuniary constraints since all would be funded by the Board. She was – yes, tempted. For a moment Marie saw herself as temptress, tried on the expression, the face. No, not with Anne. Saranjit Singh had an extremely clear idea of what he wanted and what would tempt him. Men are so practical, so shortsighted. Women see further, see where the paths divide. Or may divide.

She glanced at the photographs in the old-fashioned silver frames, which usually hid themselves behind the flowers, but there was Bobbo peeking out from under a rose spray. There was also a handful of early cherries from her garden; she had picked them at sun-up, one or two birdpecked, but why not? Bobbo. The only man she'd married. Though briefly. A wonderful choreographer, sweet-tempered, considering everything, but men, yes, men are always a little disgusting unless totally clothed. Fortunately Edmund had never made a pass at her; he had given her a couple of valuable investment tips, why? Had his reasons, probably wanting to use her for – what? Anne? But he hadn't known about Anne. Most likely only wanting to get a special hold on anyone whom he might some day want to manipulate. She nodded at Bobbo, dead for two decades, poor pet, but the life he led! And wanted her to lead. But no. Choreography was manipulation certainly, but cleaner than dear Edmund's. In fact she thought she knew what he was up to. The Board is the nice face of the Corporation, but our clever Edmund has two faces. She put a couple of cherries into her mouth, sucked them and spat out the stones, as though at the Chairman.

She shook herself, decided to video – which? One of her fellow board members. Perhaps Alberto. Not a scientist and not always for that matter apparently serious, but in some way, yes, curiously understanding of the finer points. Unlike Professor Ferguson. She made the call, was even welcomed. He had of course seen the report on their visit. 'What is she like – truly – this woman, this Anne Tomlin?'

'You didn't gather that?'

'From the report? Ah, well. But from you, my dear signora – please!'

She wasn't having it! 'Alberto – go jump in the sea! This is serious. Anne Tomlin is serious. So I think is Saranjit Singh but I am less certain. This set of discoveries of theirs they are only now beginning to understand. They have been immersed in their laboratory problems, their technique. Now they see that it is necessary to look further. And they are a little afraid.'

'Of us?'

'Undoubtedly. And perhaps they are right. They are innocent as learned people are innocent of the real world. They think they understand the impact of what they have done. One part of it at least: to feed the hungry, all the hungry. Which is, they think, a great gesture towards freedom.'

'But surely it is. the Board has agreed – '

'Freedom for what? To exchange one kind of human misery for another? When they are fed they will start wanting things. Other things. Wanting, wanting. And that is what we on the Board know.'

'Yes, indeed. Otherwise we would not be able to give these scientists so much that they want. The big institutes. The so expensive equipment. Research going on, the new discoveries! Oh yes, truly. Which without money, our money, would not happen. And that money will come from the profits on the new wants of the once hungry. It is clear.'

'Oh, totally. So they are tempted. They will fall. And people will go on wanting.'

'But to want food is the worst. Food for the wife, the children. And no food there. That is bad, bad. Perhaps you have never seen – '

'I have certainly seen. In the old days and in more places than one. It is one reason why I have preferred to be rich. So I suppose all our plans go on.'

'Edmund will see to that. So sure, so amusing, how I like to listen. Ah, I love Edmund!'

And I, she thought, love Anne. And where are we taking her? But if not the Board perhaps some slow moving international body which would probably not offer so much help and which could possibly do just as much harm. Or even, if they got to hear in time, one of the Internationals only out for quick profit. Whereas the Board – yes, even Edmund, even the Chairman, has ideas that cannot totally be measured in money. Professor Ferguson. Dr Schulman. Old Lady Martin who hardly speaks now but a great name once. They would see that the right thing was done. And it would mean, yes, she thought, it will certainly mean close contact with the scientists. With Anne. Everything was working out for the best. 'And so,' she said, 'what else did you think of our report?'

'Very interesting. Yes, extremely interesting. The detail. I am still fascinated by those two, the man and the woman. I wonder how they do this work.'

'Perhaps I can tell you a little. Anne Tomlin said to me once, and I remember exactly the very words: "The possibilities have been there always. We simply stirred and they became visible. We didn't intend it. In fact we intended, as I recollect, to find out something different.' And then this Anne laughed a little and said 'Who could have guessed that stirring an egg yolk into olive oil would turn into mayonnaise? Or even that dropping an egg onto a frying pan or more likely a hot stone would make it into something so different?' Yes, that was what she said to me.'

'Ah' said Alberto. 'You have kept in your mind, or shall I say your heart, exactly what she said, Marie. The very words. And after that you held her hand perhaps?'

'Perhaps' said Marie.

'I understand, and now before we finish I must tell you, for I too am so happy. I have just acquired a little property close to Fiesole. I shall grow my own grapes. Pears, apricots, artichokes, petit pois, everything. You must come and see.'

'But you will not want to now – when every kind of fruit and vegetable will be showered on us, perhaps too much!'

'Nonsense, mia cara,' he said. 'A good pear tree takes ten years to come into bearing, an olive twice as long. These cereals do not interest me. Let them have bread. I shall have cake.'

'But you will not leave the Board?'

'Not yet. Not yet. There are many things to consider. One or two especially – this secretariat of ours – they keep us working. Perhaps that too is for the best.'

For a little they talked about gardens. The necessity for a resting period. Varieties of wine grape. They spoke of carnations and once of the curious limestone flora of the Burgundy valley, the limestone which had to be so carefully altered in her garden. But the thought of Anne was becoming more and more pressing. They said goodbye. How long would it be before she dared video Anne, perhaps risk interrupting her at work? – no, not yet. Anne who had taught her – but she too, she would be able to teach Anne certain things.

# CHAPTER FOUR

Neil Ritchie grunted and tugged at the pipe; the water gushed again normally. He walked down along the narrow gravel path between the tanks. The two young men, Fred and Mick, who had not been allowed to help with fixing the pipe, glanced at one another and followed him. Fred was carrying a rather tatty briefcase filled with papers which their boss couldn't apparently be induced to bother about. Mick was carrying a piece of apparatus. At the fourth tank he said rather loudly: 'Hold on, Neil, shouldn't we test?'

The boss looked round. 'Do if you like. I can see.'

'Well,' said Mick doubtfully, glanced at Fred and shrugged his shoulders. At another tank Neil Ritchie slightly moved the covering shield, bent over and appeared to be smelling carefully, then slapped a fly which was exploring his neck. He was wearing a battered old straw hat; oddly enough he was sensitive about the bald patch on his head. After considering the smell he pulled one leaf out of the plants in the tank, put it in his mouth, chewed and seemed pleased. It was not a very interesting plant, but definitely edible. And outside the tanks nothing at all. And now, apparently, the boss was writing to this outfit in India about designing him a special plant. Could you believe it? Yet it did seem that the PAX mob was hooked on the same story. So what?

Judith-Ann ran down from the main building, tight pants, blue check shirt open on white throat. 'I've had this cable. He ought to answer!'

'Cable! But why don't they bloody video?' said Mick, and kicked at the gravel.

'He refused to accept' she said, and grinned. 'I was there once. A row! Smashed the viewing panel, cut his finger. I did it up. Of course it healed in no time, always does.'

'Silly old bastard! But why?'

'You want to know, mate?'

'Reason I asked.'

'Well, he's against a lot of things that weren't there when he was a kid. You know the trouble when we want a decent bit of new equipment – '

'You're telling me!'

They all laughed but there was a bit of annoyance at the back of it. He had sometimes insisted on their making things themselves. With their hands. As he did.

'Unless he's designed it himself,' Mick muttered, remembering those two models. Yes, he even blew the glass and did it rather well.

Judith-Ann went on. 'Well, same with video which is cheap, easy. But you can't hide the same way. Not that he'd mind the Board knowing what he thought of them. But it isn't private. And he wants to keep his mind to himself. He liked video to start with, so I've heard, used to jump out on people with it. A kind of toy. Then he took against it, wouldn't use it, said it stopped him thinking.'

'Bloody intuition!' That was Fred, scowling.

30

'If you like. Or just his way of thinking about thinking. But look at this, all this.' The tanks, and beyond.

Yes, yes, they were so used to it they had forgotten how impressive it was, how extraordinary and all coming out of these scribbles and graphs, these sets of figures and half of them on the backs of envelopes or other people's manuscripts. And when he was pleased you'd hear him singing away, about as much idea of a tune as a wombat!

'Yes,' said Judith-Ann, 'he's a great man. We wouldn't work with him otherwise.'

'You would, chick!' said Fred, with just a nip of jealousy in his voice.

'If you think I haven't tried!' she snorted.

'Always the big game hunter.' She turned abruptly; it had been a bit of a let down. Right. One has to take these things as they come. Or don't come.

'Go on then, take him the bloody cable!' said Mick. But for a moment more all three stood staring as they had done so often, out past the tanks, over the sand and the shimmer, feeling the hot angry sun. But the plants, the chlorophyll-rich green and now not only their first rather unpalatable fat leaves – yes, it did appear that the next stage could almost be economically harvestable. For stock feed perhaps. But would cattle or sheep drink the water they'd been grown in? Or was there a further stage? They went around with these question marks and big Neil didn't, like, see his way to answer, not yet.

Then Judith-Ann pushed past and the boys saw her touch his arm and the snappy way he turned on her. But he did read the cable. And he did wave his arms angrily the way they knew and then turn and go striding back past them as they flattened themselves against the low wall of the tank. 'Looks like he's going,' said Judith-Ann, 'cross old bastard!'

'Well,' said Mick, 'may as well test. I don't believe in my eyes – not personally – not that much.'

'Or your nose, or your bloody tongue,' said Fred, 'Might as well be a bloody stud bull as him!'

'Could be,' said Judith-Ann, 'we may be feeding stud bulls yet.' And Mick, looking up from his test, nodded.

For indeed it was impressive. At last to get a desalination plant which ingeniously used so little energy of the normal expensive kind and then to find the right vegetation for it. The final tanks were sand, irrigated with the water which had once been salt surf, powerful and beautiful. But now it was tamed, not quite drinkable, though acceptable to certain plants, trickling to their roots through pin-perforated tubes. So that the question of nutrients was the most urgent. Good old Neil. Hell to work for but all the same –

'What was the cable then?' said Fred.

'You'd be surprised,' said Judith-Ann. 'Or maybe you won't. But it was from PAX all right. They asked him to video back – reversed charges. He likes that. Takes his time.'

'One of their bloody conferences,' said Fred. 'Old Neil isn't too keen.'

'Yes, but who with?' said Judith-Ann, tossing back a real old tease of a look.

'Let me guess,' said Mick, looking up from the tank. 'Is it Herb's crowd?'

'Just that,' said Judith-Ann, 'the Yanks. And it seems they've got something we could grow in bulk – one genuine new nitrogen fixer! That would be something, that sure would.'

'That bloody would,' said Fred, and then, to Mick: 'This story, about that mob in India designing us a plant – sounds a lot of cock. Right?'

32

'There've been stories,' said Mick, 'something the Boss was saying about plants that could mop up the Na and Cl – '

'And give us back pure $H^2O$! Sorry, I'm not taking any.'

'Grow water melons full of the good stuff, keep the rest in their leaves!' said Judith-Ann. 'Melons bursting at regular intervals.'

'By the Boss's gold watch! Best S.F. stuff!' They all giggled, then Mick said: 'All the same I've heard they got some striking results at this Centre. Bloody striking. I wouldn't put anything past them.'

'Ah, come off it, mate!' They looked at one another and went back to the main building. It was sweaty weather right enough. Beaut little beads on Judith-Ann's low cut.

Back inside in the air conditioning they could hear old Neil shouting at the video operator and glanced at one another. Mick was making some notes. Judith-Ann looked out of the big window over the tanks, the shielded and the unshielded. Beyond the tanks lay long bare miles of unusable enemy sand, the edge of the great Australian central desert, the immense ancient dried out sea which yet might change out of all knowledge.

'How do you see it, Mick?' she said. 'Grazing stock bulls, riding horses, putting up wire fences, killing off kangaroos, the old lot?'

'No,' said Mick, 'but maybe – if it was possible to get, you know, some kind of beans, or even a cereal, so we could feed ourselves, all Australia.'

'If we could get water – our water – on to all that out there we'd feed more than Australia. Millions more.'

'And who would profit?' said Fred. 'You know, Judith. Bloody PAX.'

'Unless they could cut their profits – so it would be cheap,

33

could feed, oh, all those kind of people outside – if they could be induced.'

'False,' said Fred, snorting.

'Not necessarily,' Judith-Ann said. 'After all – it would look well, and an outfit like PAX needs to have an image. They've even got something written into their registration or whatever it's called. The good of mankind: all that cock.'

'Just what it is! Come off it, girl, be your age – we all know PAX is the same as the rest of the bloody mob.'

'That's exactly what we don't know, young Fred. Could be they might just now be considering something in the nature of free food – at least for some people. Listen now, you silly clot! These Abos, the ones up on the camp site, they could do with feeding.'

'Lazy swine!'

'Have a heart Fred,' said Mick. 'Those Abos don't see the bloody point of the sort of work they can get. The stock-men are O.K. And they're interested in machines when some of us take the trouble to explain. Yes, if PAX was to feed them –'

'And anyway,' said Judith-Ann, 'it's good old PAX who've been supporting us.'

'In the manner we're accustomed to,' said Mick and went to the cupboard at the back of the big centrifuge and took out glasses and an Orlando Riesling from Barossa. Old Neil had stamped off into what he called his study, leaving them, not telling them anything, not him! 'To us!' said Mick, and put an arm round Judith-Ann, feeling for her breasts where the sweat was cooling off and finding himself only minimally pushed away. Not bad. Nor the Riesling.

# CHAPTER FIVE

It all seems to take a long time but there are natural processes which cannot be hurried beyond a certain point. Once the deicate manipulation had been achieved and tested, families of clones had to be developed. The techniques were sometimes difficult, but gradually they became more or less standardized. New problems and little triumphs constantly turned up, fascinating; months lapsed into years and letters got shoved aside. Saranjit Singh looked across at Anne. Yes, she had her F.R.S. now. He was not at all jealous; he had so much else. And she – what?

It was the coffee break in the big room. Several of the staff were there already, but were mostly gathered at the far end round the biscuits and sambals. There was dark hair and fair hair, even a red; younger colleagues had arrived and there were almost too many visitors these days. Beyond the big table there was a door half open into a normally messy room with bits of glassware on the table and papers on the floor: work, clearly, in progress. At the far side a red light showed over another door: something going on there too. Along the main window there was a range of leaves from woolly to glossy in various stages of growth, some shaded, others with coloured filters across the light. Measurement notes were pinned up on the wall, graphs with the sudden jumps and the date and time marked in, drawings and a few photos, a memo. Outside two of the students were preparing an experimental trench with a transistor radio on the ground beside them, but turned fairly low; they'd be along in a few minutes, hungry; they probably hadn't had any breakfast.

Looking at Anne, Saranjit caught himself actually seeing her. Inevitably they looked at one another as they pushed bits

of paper across: diagrams, calculations or micro photographs, or when they crossed glances, worried or excited over growing plants. But if he really saw her there were the white hairs coming, the extra little lines on her skin, almost as brown as his now, but not taking the sun easily. Never. No more than her grandfather, the judge, the great shot, the great cricketer, more than that, the great gardener whom he just remembered, had ever taken the Indian sun easily. He too had been browned and wrinkled, the eye-lids coming down, narrowing the look. The hawk look. He and his grand-daughter could almost have passed for Northerners, Pathans. But the blue of the eyes gave them away.

When they had first started working together, Anne must have been in her early thirties, her hair short and glossy brown, a touch of gold. But was she pretty? He didn't know; he had been in the excitememnt of his own marriage to Nandu, the perfection of her fine-arched brows, the glow of her eyes and the long enveloping wave of hair. Nandu who was so beautiful still in her splendid motherliness! But now poor Anne was looking very tired.

She ought to take a holiday. Not a conference, a real break. She said she hadn't liked England when she was back there staying with her sister. So no, England was not very comfortable these days. Nor was India. But differently; at least there were still servants – that there would be so long as there was hunger. The thing that might be dealt with, at last. And then? Yes, Anne could ask her sister to stay with her in some comfortable hotel somewhere; they existed. And perhaps she would also amuse herself in that way of hers of which he did not quite approve. Yes, yes. There was enough money in the project from several sources, including the first PAX grants. And yet, if they said yes to these new PAX proposals, there would be more. Almost unbelievably more. Enough for the whole scale of things to change. But Anne would not even travel first class. He always did – now. However, they ought to answer these letters. Instead of putting it off week after week. Anne had not much liked the first proposals from the Board; they had different ideas from hers of what social morality was about. She had even written to F.A.O. but the letter had met with no enthusiastic response. 'Anne' he said, 'let us at once try to decide what to do.'

'We can't sell ourselves,' she said. They were speaking quietly, not overheard; her lab coat was frayed at the edges. His was new, gleaming white, as was his turban. Underneath his eyes looked all the darker, but worried now about her.

'But we shall not sell ourselves.' He had tried to explain this before. 'We shall go on working on the project. Not for them. However much we send them in reports. Which need not trouble us too much. And we can take in further lines, you know – some of the things we have been discussing, Anne. For the sake of all that we shall find out, you know. The advancement of human knowledge.' She shifted her head irritably. 'Oh, all right,' he said, 'because we want to!'

'There will be pressure,' said Anne wearily 'Pressure of some kind, in spite of what Marie-Claire says.' She took off her spectacles and dropped them.

He picked them up and wiped them on his spotless silk handkerchief. She almost never wore silk, he nowadays almost always. Why not? 'There are always pressures of one kind or another. I am so sure we can cope. Look, my dear Anne, if we don't go in with these people we shall be bothered and interrupted by dozens of others. You know what it's been like ever since our work has become known. These ones are the best, not just because they wish to appear philanthropic, perhaps genuinely so, but because they are a very big International, too big for standard cheating, and they will protect us from the others. The PAX board want to make money, yes, and a large part of it will go to our outfit which we shall use exactly as we think fit. Look at the large scale trials we shall be having, on different soils. Different climates. Outside the Sub-Continent, you know. And we have been promised no silly ideas from them, no constraints. And after all, they have agreed with the main thing. No patents on the scientific side. If everything works out as we believe it will, they are going to feed the world: free.'

'It's in the letters, I know. And Marie-Claire promised it would be all right. But I don't entirely trust Sir Edmund. And some of the others.'

'It's going to be tied up. And public. Their profits are not to come out of that little thing, food. PAX is into – oh everything! Look, Anne, we have the best lawyers, Hindus and Christians though they are. We pay them to keep us right. If we go on and on worrying about it, we can't work, either of us. And after all, nitrogen fixation in cereals is real. And Ritchie in Australia. Then of course the geneticists, though I cannot think they will have a happy time with our plants. But they want to try.'

'Americans are always in such a hurry. One has to stop and think.'

'Haven't you thought plenty, my dear Anne? What about your long talks with the Raffray?'

'Marie-Claire. Ah, but that was different. I was teaching her, explaining. And then, we talked of – other things.' Anne seemed to relax a little, remembering. Her mouth quivered perceptibly.

38

Saranjit took a deep breath. So that was how it had been! Yes, of course. But so fortunate that she did not allow herself to be at all deflected. 'Anne, you are a strange girl. Not that I mind who you go to bed with. Or whatever it is you do. Though I wish for your sake it had been a man.'

'For my sake – why?' She did not bother to be embarrassed.

'You would have had more pleasure. At least with a good man.'

But Anne shook her head slowly. 'Marie-Claire came, I have no doubt, only to discuss our future. From the Board. We had a certain amount of discussion. Useful discussion, as you know. She was willing to learn, that is so important. Then in the course of it we became interested in one another. Differently. It was a hot day and you know how much I dislike air conditioning. We needed to relax. I found out a great deal about her: happily. Ah, well, it makes no difference and I feel the better for it. Marie-Claire will certainly be visiting us again.'

'I suppose we were correct, yes, sensible to go no further with, well, the entirely respectable bodies. Or so we think of them. You know, Anne, F.A.O. and so on. I know you were disappointed with their answer. I also.'

'It would have been impossible to work with them – all those regulations and which country one has to get one's supplies from! It would tie us even worse. All that ridiculous paper. They would want to plan everything themselves. Their own experts! No, this PAX thing will at least not try that on us. I made this entirely clear to Marie-Claire.'

'And she accepted – on behalf of this Board of theirs?'

'Of which she is an important member. Oh yes. She understands: completely.'

'So you agree that we are going to – to help, you know, to feed all those who are hungry?'

She looked away, not answering; the silence grew. It seemed as if she was merely looking at a wire and plaster model she had once made herself, a set of curious interlacings. The rest of the staff had left. There was only a faint, not unpleasing smell of coffee and spices in the big room. Saranjit waited, relaxed, as one might wait in a temple for something to happen.

But were they doing the right thing? Yes, yes, no doubt. To feed the world. The old, old dream. It had been in all religions, all great stories. But was food enough to change people's feelings towards one another? Or was this always and only done by working together? 'Anne,' he said, 'I think you should take a break. Soon. You were telling me you had heard of some aberrant plant form in Australia. Why don't we say yes to these people and then you could go and look for it? At the same time you could see how Ritchie is getting on in his desert or whatever it is now. That could be interesting. Look, why don't you take my Rahul? He is quite bright for a fourteen year old, you know, and he would carry your bags. And I guarantee he wouldn't interrupt. As a matter of fact he thinks the world of you. Much more than he does of me, his own father! But we ought to decide first about our answer to PAX.'

She looked up suddenly. 'All right, Saranjit. If they're really going to do it. For the hungry world. We must.'

# CHAPTER SIX

So here she was, after all, in Australia, out of reach of the worries and, as they fell away, more able to think clearly. Yes, it had been a good idea, going off for this part-working holiday with Rahul. The Centre had got the tickets, reminded her about innoculations and saw to it that there was a clean page in her passport for the Australian visa, though why they should be so fussy – ! 'It's because of all this guilt about the aboriginals' said Saranjit. 'They have to find themselves a clean sheet. India – Bangla Desh – Indonesia – Campuchea, we don't have to worry about our guilt, it's quite the thing, so we don't need a clean page.' Anne had laughed, but perhaps it was true. The guilt was official. But we, she thought, will ship in Freefood and their guilt will be ended. At least that was how it looked in Darwin.

But Darwin and the Institute where they were temporary guests was only the beginning. Their hosts in Darwin had warned them about their journey into Arnhem Land. 'You see,' said one of the sociologists, they wouldn't take on the old name, couldn't expect that, could we? Well, this newest state in Australia is to be called – and I'm sure we wish them well – Murngin, after one of the tribal groups. Not even the biggest, but there you are. Kind of accident.'

'How interesting!' said Anne. 'I hadn't realized. Are they doing well?'

'Seems they're trying to think up some form of government which would be at least –' he smiled a little, ' – recognizable. But so far, well, some of their notions will have to change. There are a few stock farms which have been handed over; seems they're managing them all right. Well, we'll need to see.'

'Are the boundaries fixed?' Anne asked.

'Not altogether. Those clots in Queensland are fighting their end. Ought to be bloody pleased to get rid of some of their Abos. They could be a no-good mob but they got treated in a no-good way in Queensland. You can't do that and get away with it. No. You'll have no trouble at the border. Not yet!'

Nor did they. Driving east, at first through cattle country, they came to various groups of painted signs, clearly about the new State. Some were in English, others appeared to have symbols of some kind. But there was no obvious border. No doubt that could wait. Meanwhile Rahul had to be introduced to the world of tree ferns and then of cycads, and also along the coast to mangrove swamps, so interesting and for that matter so beautiful once you get over the literary associations. He knew something already of the semi-tropics and had a good eye for odd orchids, but he became commendably excited by the dry-land flora. How much of northern Australia was dry, apparently accommodating only a few species! Until you looked closer. Rahul, Anne was glad to see, had begun to look and often to find. His botanical drawing, cramped at first, was expanding and getting in the significant detail. He was certainly going to be bright on the recognition level. That was no proof that he was a budding scientist, but she was watching him. What an old hen I'm being, she thought to herself. His fuss about retying his turban was simply niggling, but the careful stamen count and the skilful use of the mini-microscope, that seemed to be all right. Was it going to interfere that he seemed to take religion so seriously? He had stood up rather well to a bit of ribbing from some beer-drinking biologists in Darwin. I shan't criticize, she said to herself, not yet. Let him use being

42

a Sikh as his steady point in this difficult business of growing up.

They went on, careful of their map readings, firmly resting through the heat. They had a good little truck, specialized for this type of work. Anne often let Rahul drive; after all he knew far more about engines than either she or his father, and nobody in the middle of nowhere was going to ask his age. On the whole they had seen very few other people in the last four or five days, since moving out of the cattle country. They had both admired the aboriginal stock-men, marvellous riders but not easy to communicate with. 'They don't want to talk' said Rahul, 'it's mostly you, Anne, being white. I'm trying to explain. You're not really white inside.'

'How do you mean, Rahul? Our only contact is a few utility words. Nothing you can do any explaining with!'

'I don't quite know,' he said, 'but somehow I've got an idea.' He had his hand over – yes, probably a nerve centre – but wasn't that just an accidental gesture? She watched the fingers, the slender brown boy's hand, contracting as if something had to be grasped. 'I don't think – perhaps,' he said, frowning, 'it's just words. I think really – it's more inside, Anne. I am – you know – learning it. Anyway if it can get learned, that's what I want to do. As well as botany!'

As they got further out into the north-east they met an occasional family group of Aboriginals, mostly, it seemed to Anne, in poor shape. But if, yes, if this Freefood idea really gets off the ground, we'll be feeding this crowd. The next lot of babies are more likely to survive. But what for? What future? All this talk in Darwin about a genuine new Aboriginal state in the north. Not just an area of land which nobody else wanted, but something with development possibilities, water – and perhaps a legislature of some kind, the Aboriginals living under their own rules. Of course there had been a lot of disapproval, though not from the Institute, but it would lift that nasty old load of guilt!

So if they were fed? Nobody was thinking along those lines. How far ahead must we look for the outcome of a piece of research? Like all scientists she thought briefly about atomic history. Looked away. The worst hadn't happened. Not yet. Perhaps it wouldn't – not ever.

It was so nice, so restful, to watch Rahul rushing about, looking for things, all excited. There had been times when she had wished for a child of her own, but was that genuine? She loved Rahul and Rahul loved her. And oh how funny he was about Neil Ritchie! Gorgeous to have someone to laugh with. He was an experimenter already, had an accurate visual and tactile memory. He found taxonomy amusing instead of boring. And he washed his own clothes.

By now they were camping near a curiously sited water hole in one of those extraordinary orange cliffs that seem to burst out of the Australian deserts. There was a cleft with dark water, clearly not permanent, but still out of depth for a swimmer, even a little alarming. Anne had intended at first to camp quite close by, but then realized that they might be interfering with those for whom it was not a holiday place, but something culturally essential; she would go no further in assessing the probabilities.

In fact since they had been there they had seen several groups of Aboriginals or single people; twice someone had come up to them and there had been at least an attempt at conversation. Anne had been delighted at the small, quaint foreigness of Australia and had gone native with a genuine billy of tea over a brushwood fire. She was also trying out ways of enlivening a damper. When these visitors came she had handed out cups of tea, well sugared. Rahul kept trying out the few words he knew, though it was not clear that all the visitors had the same speech. One of the men had shown him how to throw a spear.

Again, Anne had been worried about the women and children; the babies seemed to do well enough, but later on there were signs of protein deficiency. So we've got to get the Freefood to this lot, she thought, oh, we shall feed them! Yet she wasn't quite sure. She handed out slices of damper and jam to some of the kids, who licked off the jam. Once one of the women brought some roots and made signs that she should cook them in the ashes; so she did and they tried some; they were certainly edible, though not exactly nice. Still, she pretended and got the woman to show her the plant, apparently one of the araceae. If you liked that, you probably didn't like wheaten bread, so why push it? Had that a moral for Freefood?

One way and another Anne kept wondering whether these wanderers might have been pushed off a better environment. The white Australian guilt feeling was quite wide-spread, but had not gone as far as returning prosperous ranches. But one must remember it was not only Australians who were involved, but outsiders, Vesteys and such. So, if there was to be this Aboriginal State they were talking about in Darwin, what then? Oh well, she couldn't let herself get involved with other people's politics.

Rahul had gone for water to the gully in the cliffs and came back looking worried, for a time not wanting to speak. At last he said: 'Anne, I don't like to speak of this. Perhaps I was dreaming. But it did seem, well, to be real.'

'Go on,' she said, 'we're always getting surprizes.'

'Well, there was this man who came past me, very quietly,

you know, like they do. He was painted. I wish I knew what that meant. And something like – I don't know what – on his head. He was fairly close. He knelt down on the flat stone and took a drink of the water, his face right into it, not palmed up. I think he had seen me, I'm not sure. And then – '

'Then?' Anne asked. Rahul had screwed up his eyes, twisted his head away.

'Well, then he just wasn't there any more. Like that.'

'You were watching him?'

'Yes. He was there. I could hear him lapping. He stood up from the water. And then, then there was nobody there. Anne, I don't believe in magic!'

'Everything's magic till we understand it,' said Anne, 'and there's a lot we don't understand yet. Don't worry.'

'But could it have happened? Really?'

'Almost anything can happen or appear to happen. Anyhow it was harmless. You know, Rahul, perhaps this water hole has been used for thousands of years. Long, long before our time. What they call "the dreaming".'

'Do you mean, Anne, could I have seen something from – then?'

'Well, there are theories about time folds. And about places where things have happened that leave some kind of trace that can be picked up by the right person. Who might be you. It's not my field, you know. And it's nothing to be frightened about.'

He seemed to relax more or less. She opened a tin of chicken and vegetables; it was what Rahul liked. All the tins they used were scoured with sand and then put carefully into one place behind a rock, not left lying about. She had signed to one of the passing women to take one; the word might go round and after they had left, looking for a new camp site in an area with different flora, the tins might find a use.

Later in the day Anne made a note in her diary. But she hoped Rahul might forget or at least put it down to some momentary lack of attention. A dream. The dreaming. What are dreams?

# CHAPTER SEVEN

Some of the Board's ideas were worth following up and provided new contacts which, in turn, set new ideas in train. Two of the staff from the Centre had gone over to Australia to discuss with Neil Ritchie the type of plant which could be usefully grown. There was a perceptible shift towards trying for an increase of protein first, and then perhaps of other valuable properties, all of which would increase world health. But so much work goes on all over the world – something often discussed in some obscure journal that one doesn't notice, but it fits. Suddenly it's important. 'What exactly is this nutrition expert they are sending over up to? What are we going to be involved in next?' said Anne, frowning a little.

'Building in carotene, I believe. Perhaps in some of the roots. But one idea is to have green vegetables parcelled in with the free rice.'

'And a picture of celebrities eating it or they'll still think it's poor man's food. This wretched rice!'

'It's not rice everywhere, after all. We can work with the

colocasias; they should be easy. Easier than the amaranths. Roots should be no more of a problem than any other part. It's a case of the auxins surely.'

'I'm not convinced. We've been able to build in more proteins, but roots aren't leaves. After all, the real breakthrough was with the chloroplasts. Saranjit, I don't think we have quite understood what we think we can do. And we certainly mustn't let ourselves be bullied by PAX. We don't necessarily know how root structures react.' More time, thought Anne, more time!

Saranjit nodded. 'There are those two papers which I think we should take into account, Anne.'

'I know. But I have some worries. I would prefer to check on their results myself.'

'Yes. But it would take time.'

'And they're trying to hurry us, as usual. A new idea and they have to rush at it! Root reactions are bound to have differences which we don't understand yet and which may not appear immediately.'

'Indeed yes, Anne, indeed! But new problems are surely the greatest of pleasures. No?'

Anne laughed and shook her head. Bio-engineering certainly had all the fascination you could ask for and Saranjit was sparkling like a boy. But life has this odd way of jumping back at you. Those two papers – one of them very brilliant and from, so to speak, their own stable. But all the same essential to verify. 'Well,' she said, 'we'd better make a plan.'

'It will certainly mean a year's work, at least. Yes, yes, we must have a firm basis. But I am most sure, Anne, that we shall end with improved roots.'

'So long as they don't go aberrant in some way. Toxicities.

Perhaps we should go on with the new rice; there is still room for improvement.'

'I think that too,' said Saranjit. 'Also I do not think the rice eaters will accept anything else, not yet anyhow. I know my own people. So, it is harder to change human nature than to make – our kind of change.'

'The same with taro eaters, I suppose. Do you know this nutrition expert who is coming, Saranjit? We have corresponded but – I suppose the Z stands for Zacharias, one of those crazy Bible names they still go on with in America.'

'Actually,' said Saranjit, 'it stands for Zeenat. I believe she came originally from a Moslem family. Yes, Zeenat, a pretty name.' He looked from under his brows at Anne and smiled a little. Her weakness! She had looked for a moment delightfully flustered and less than her age.

Anne enquired around about carotene, thought about the colocasias and, for that matter, the yams in general, all of which, apparently, had to be cooked or otherwise processed to get rid of unpleasant poisons. Cassava root was low in almost everything, as useless as cooking plantains for anything except bulk, and this should soon be a thing of the past. The green cassava tops were fine, but the eaters didn't stuff themselves as the root eaters did. It would be tricky to do this building in of protiens, the Board were so keen on. There were times when she simply wanted to leave the root crops alone; surely it was enough to have done so much on the cereals and legumes? But the Board were keen to help over Polynesia and Melanesia. The Centre could always refuse, on good grounds. There would be no come-back. But all the same ... She and Saranjit meanwhile had long videos with some of the geneticists.

The nutrition expert arrived. Would she be – what, what?

49

But no. Zeenat Jonsens's visit could not have been more strictly professional. She was small, brisk, spectacled, notebooked. She had married a Moslem Swedish-American psychologist who took the Koranic precepts very seriously, feeling perhaps that what he needed was a really rigid mainmast to keep a grip on. He carried a prayer mat and kept his head covered, thus keeping in step with those members of the older stem of monotheism, amongst whom he had several colleagues. Zeenat herself was less religiously demanding, though naturally she drew some lines, especially those consistent with her work as a respected nutritionist.

She was staying with Saranjit and Nandu who were used to such things, though as Sikhs they found all religions had some good in them, some bad. The formalities were of no genuine moral import but should be adhered to. For instance, Saranjit's hair billowed down to his knees when he unfolded his turban; he laughed at himself but yet he had a certain secret pride which perhaps helped and steadied him when, for example, he got into the frustrating work snags which were bound to happen from time to time. All the symbols of Sikhdom helped, touching the sense of historic courage. His fingers would creep onto the dagger or the bracelet and he would feel that help was coming his way, power from – somewhere – pouring into him. What had Anne got which gave her the same confidence? The pure sense of scientific achievement? No, no, that could melt away. Her family, above all her grandfather, the man about whom all the stories were told and retold? The maker of the great garden? But did she think in the same way? And was she sad to have no children of her own? He often wondered about this. Yet she was fond of many of the younger people and took endless trouble to help them with their papers, to encourage them or, more difficult, if what they were trying to express was nonsense, to tell them so kindly.

Saranjit and Nandu were happy with their marriage and their family. Their own elder son was by now at university but his main interest was films, not that it was anything but an intelligent and informed interest. But Saranjit felt that the younger one, Rahul, was really nearer to being a scientist. A scientist and a Sikh because that also mattered. It had made a real difference to him, that month in Australia with Anne. And yes, he thought it had made a difference to Anne herself. The boy was already good at watching things, collecting facts and letting them talk to him and he saw what mathematics was about. He was always coming over to see Anne and ask questions; she didn't seem to mind.

The girls were of course being educated but had so far shown no special talents. Difficult for a pretty and highly marriageable Indian girl to be quite serious about a career. Anne scolded him for giving them silks and jewellery instead of books. But, said Saranjit, they had enough money to buy books for themselves and why must she deprive him of the pleasure of giving what he enjoyed choosing and what they so much enjoyed getting?

A great deal of Zeenat Jonsen's information was very interesting. For the first day or so Anne felt herself sufficiently repelled by Zeenat's somewhat unexpected personality to pay as much attention as she recognized was due to the importance of this colleague. She used, Anne thought, an undue amount of scent, too obvious, as though to cover something less pleasant. Whereas Marie-Claire's was a delightful enhancement of what was already there. However it was necessary to get over such unimportant matters, as there was much serious business to discuss. For instance,

51

neither Saranjit nor Anne had completely realized the nutritional distinctions between the different mangoes, the rajakeena, the shepu and so on. Essential to go for the yellow-fleshed. But trees take time, can probably be left to private enterprise although some experimental work would be in order and, for that matter, quite enjoyable. But the Board for whom Zeenat worked in her advisory capacity were particularly keen on the grams, pulses and dahls, though she agreed whole-heartedly with the Board that many of the African and Polynesian root-crops needed considerable alteration. Some of this looked genetically possible, but might not work out. Nitrogen fixation had got nowhere with the sweet potato, but there was always the possibility of a breakthrough. It could well be that the Centre here could help; there were possibilities of careful morphogenesis; what happens in the leaf affects everything. Zeenat spent the whole of the afternoon with Anne, mostly among the graphs and measurements; like most other women, including Marie-Claire, she was fascinated by the sets of micro-tools, so pretty, so delicate! However, they went out after the usual afternoon rain had cooled down air and foliage, to visit some of the actual plants. Some of them were indeed remarkable and unexpected.

'We have had to be cautious,' Anne said, 'you're correct in assuming that our experiments in morphogenesis sometimes went wrong. In fact we had one or two almost alarming results. Others were – just funny.' They were looking at a tiny banana which was one such result but so charming in its way that they had cloned a few for the front of the border.

'Yes, yes, leaf is all. In a sense we are all made of leaves.'

'Perhaps,' said Anne uncertainly. The rather obscure word phyllomania, used by an Indian colleague, drifted through her mind. Too many leaves, yes, well –

'Leaves carrying the protein message throughout the plant' said Zeenat; her spectacles were aglitter and her bosom heaved. 'When we think of all these awakened leaves with their choloroplasts busily fabricating! The vitamins. The carotene. How fortunate you have been that nothing has gone wrong!'

'So far,' said Anne quickly.

'Imagine the possible molecular combinations which might have appeared – even in the ovules!'

'We have been able to predict with reasonable accuracy,' Anne said, 'once the auxins were sorted out. All the same, we have some anxieties about our projected work on root systems. As you know, these roots are not only the staple food in some cultures, but also carry definite toxins.'

'But surely these can be eliminated?'

'We hope so. But of course, our main work has been on cereals and legumes. There are various leguminous poisons, but so far no increase in the slight percentage in the ovule. We got our mathematics right. Just as well.'

'Fortunate indeed. Beautiful indeed. The work of God, with you – with us – as His instruments. And for the world.' Zeenat adjusted her spectacles and peered at a row of very splendid climbing beans; a family could feed itself for a couple of weeks on one plant; there would be ample protein.

'You feel then,' said Anne, 'that the Freefood programme really will make all that difference – socially?'

'Undoubtedly,' said Zeenat, and she really looked a little shocked at the question. 'I am surprised that there is any possible doubt on this. Look around you. Here in the east –'

'I know,' said Anne, 'but will it make all that difference elsewhere in the developed world?'

'The standard of living is measured by the shopping basket and that, as you must know, is mainly food. Though our programme will also bring down the price of, for example, soap, and of course tobacco. Not that I approve, but the leaf structure was almost too easy to work on. Even scents, I think, the very essence of leaf improvement, yet immeasurable.' She shut her eyes for a moment behind her spectacles. 'Scent, yes, that harmless addiction! The Prophet would have approved.'

'But people will want other things.'

'Naturally. And as we know, so gratefully, how Sir Edmund said at a recent meeting that the PAX board in conjunction with the Corporation were prepared to supply every need.'

'He said that, did he? Yes, I am sure we were sent a copy of the minutes. But I can't say I read everything.'

'You should always read,' said Zeenat. 'Yes, always. He is a great man, Sir Edmund, a wonderful man.'

Anne said nothing but remembered the moment when the name Zeenat had called up a brief image of someone lovely, graceful, not young, no, but ageing into a delicate elegance. Yes, elegance was what she fancied, something so far from her own style – come, come, stop thinking about Marie-Claire! After all Marie-Claire is one of the Board, one of Sir Edmund's chickens, that side of her something to be slightly wary of, although, on other levels ... but all the same and after cold consideration Anne could not suppose that Marie-Claire would ever refer to Sir Edmund as a wonderful man. Or at least not in that tone of voice.

She led the way towards a splendid rice plant, strong stemmed, heavy headed. 'But you must visit our temperate zone centre' she said. 'We use Australia mostly. There's plenty of room there and Ritchie's desalination work is

54

opening it all up. I expect they've started feeding those natives of theirs.'

'How fortunate we are,' said Zeenat, 'in our world!'

Anne felt that this was going rather far. No major war actually happening. Freefood – food for all the world – well on its way. That must be good, mustn't it? Though she had always disliked the way the world seemed to be run by monopolies. And PAX was, she supposed, the biggest. No, why should she have to think about something she couldn't alter. A fortunate world? 'Yes, perhaps at the moment' she said. Well, the visit was nearly over, the necessary purposes agreed.

# CHAPTER EIGHT

Yes indeed, the board meetings became more interesting every year. At least this was how they appeared to Sir Edmund and to some, certainly, of his colleagues. All realized that the scope of PAX was spreading and spreading, while the somewhat vague wording about the mission of capital towards world improvement which headed the quarterly reports, seemed to be becoming actualized. There was the large scale cloning, most of which now took place in various stations, some even in different climatic and soil conditions from those in the old centre where most of the manipulation still happened. There were geneticists, there were medical and health teams. The Board would always be a handsome donor, sometimes the actual source of all salaries; unlike some donors or trusts, PAX took an intimate and above all encouraging interest in all that was going on, but, remarkably, without visible interference or pressurizing. The Corporation stayed discreetly in the background, but other companies – and the most strangely varied – were acquired or amalgamated. Majority holdings of shares suddenly blossomed as the seeds sown deep underground matured and burst out into conquering bloom. The Annual Reports were discreetly optimistic, sometimes rather difficult to follow, but the photographs were outstanding. Naturally there was bargaining, demands for a seat on the Board. But much of the Board manipulation and decision-making went on well out of the comparative publicity of the boardroom itself. Some colleagues were more understanding than others. It made sense, measurable sense when measurement was in the unmistakeable terms of money.

There were difficulties of course, real setbacks sometimes, especially over energy sources. However, there were more possibilities by now than had seemed likely up to the last decade of the twentieth century. Sir Edmund was here, there and everywhere, usually with some of his technical advisers. There had been simple problems of land and water acquisition, though there were also transport problems, many of which had been solved through earlier purchases of sometimes derelict docks, containers and shipping. It was found that most governments came in, some with more safeguards than others. The Board had no objection at all to national participation, even nominal ownership if that fitted in with the politics of a particular nation. The benefits were so clear that there would seldom be any interference, only perhaps a new face at occasional Board meetings, an acceptable phrase added to reports, or a new official address to which to send copies of reports, decisions, statistics, speeches and so on.

It had for instance been willingly agreed that the Bantustans should be fed through South African agencies, though the quantity and quality per head must be up to Board standards. There was a discreet inspectorate reporting in detail only to part of the Board. Yes, the Board quite understood that it would be a disaster if the mine labour was suddenly cut off. Some Board members had been shocked at this, but once they saw what was likely to happen – and they were taken aside to have the strategy explained to them – they agreed that the approach was right. The Chairman made the necessary sympathetic noises to the politicians, but explained that the Board could not be expected to change its basic organization and must insist on totally free and adequate supplies even if the Government's name was on the bag. The South African representative on the Board was, at least in private, considerably more far-sighted than his own Government's declared policy might lead one to expect.

No doubt the general health of the natives would be improved and that could not but benefit everyone. Besides, the Chairman also suggested, it would have a very bad effect if the people of Transkei and Quazulu and so on began to realize how well the neighbouring African states were making out on Freefood; they would soon cease to act as reliable labour supplies, and then where would you be? You would be risking revolution. Better not risk it. Better to send in the Freefood under the government label and put up mine wages if they needed the workers. Indeed a general rise in wages might be sensible, though naturally PAX could only make suggestions; it was nothing to do with the Board if the South African Government labels were painted out as soon as the trucks were cleared through, and some quite other name plastered onto the corn, rice and bean sacks. People in these 'Home Lands' who had been – but of course no Board member would have said deliberately – half starved for two or three generations, were now fed and could live as families. They could take heart at last and, instead of being forced out to work in the white-ruled world, the men began to cope with their own difficult land. Yes, but it was their own, and the children began to grow up healthy and bright. In this way several almost genuine independencies came into being and small local industries began to flourish.

There were all sorts of reactions. South Australia had been quick and generous with what had always been considered as hopeless desert, once they were convinced that the great semi-desalination plants were on the drawing-board and that the crops which would thrive on this almost undrinkable water had gone through large scale tests. The whole thing had been fascinating, too, from the zoological point of view. Some kinds of marsupial could manage, both with the water and the types of grass and weeds which were likely to do best. It was perhaps fortunate that none of the non-native animals, including rabbits, seemed able to flourish. Nor did the imported bramble. And there were fascinating new varieties of pests on some of the crops. An expedition from the Monash Zoological Department had a most interesting time, working on this. One of them nearly married Judith-Ann.

Queensland was less amenable on land or indeed on the idea of Freefood. It went totally against the political philosophy, if such it could be called, of those in power. That, of course, was a problem here and there when top groups acted blindly without grasping, as the South African Government had done at first, how to work in with a totally new and upsetting situation so that they would not appear to be in opposition. It was, anyhow, really encouraging for the Board that so little had to be spent on the usual bribes almost anywhere in the world. Heads of governments often turned out to be passionately keen to feed their people, especially those with incipient revolutions. They would also avoid expensive food imports in bad years and the necessity of growing lucrative export foods instead of the cheap food crops their populations needed. Yes, food could be taken out of politics. Naturally Prime Ministers, Presidents, or for that matter Emperors, wanted public credit, but that was all right, it cost little, in fact ran itself once you gave it a push. Security and order asserted themselves always when the hungry were filled, even if the rich were not necessarily sent away empty.

The Ritchie semi-desalination technique had been successfully employed for growing the specially designed wheat in the Sinai desert. It was found a couple of years later that a local barley could also be adapted and successfully grown. The earlier American twentieth century work on cereals for this type of soil was followed up. There were plans for tree planting, which might in time influence the weather, which had been slightly deteriorating in the Northern hemisphere at least over the last twenty years. The new Japanese Board member, an R. and D. man all through, was particularly interested in this type of development and pressurized the rest of the Board to support it. It might be possible to do something for Hokesaido: Dr. Ikeya's patriotism extended to all the islands.

This Sinai scheme was being run by a mixed team of

Egyptian and Israeli technicians who got on excellently and were equally annoyed by the carelessness and inability to be on time shown by the Bedouin workers who were being employed as a deliberate matter of Board policy. The only troubles arose when there were visiting politicians; most of the media people had more sense and did not make trouble. Luckily, one of the Israelis was particularly adept at making songs which poked rather unkind fun at the politicians and gave a lot of pleasure to everyone else.

The interesting thing was that in spite of very large expenditure on Freefood, the PAX shareholders – mostly in the world-wide Corporation network of associated companies – were still getting a very reasonable dividend from other sources. And Sir Edmund was quite clear that this would continue, in fact would augment very satisfactorily once those who had been forced to spend every penny on food could instead spend on other goods, possibly with a larger profit margin and to a great extent within the PAX empire. This was explained in the happiest way, usually by Sir Edmund himself, but sometimes by Alberto who had grasped the non-scientific aspect very quickly, occasionally by Madame Raffray with her more feminine methods of producing happy agreement. Often there were large board meetings with new members appointed, on the whole showpieces from the hungry countries, for instance dear little Ethel Gabani with her curious hair-do, from that quite heavily populated Polynesian island, or the man from Eritrea who had lost his right arm in the war. A few of these expressed a certain disappointment with results on the personal level, but the PAX code was quite strict. Sir Edmund, for example, could say with perfect truth that he had never accepted a gift of which the intention was to deflect his purpose. There had been an occasional donation for one of his collections but these, he felt, were a contribution towards world aesthetics. He had already turned over those he was tired of to museums or galleries, mostly in countries which might perhaps be critical of certain aspects of PAX, and which were short on early Picassos.

So now, after so few years when you consider the millenia of human misery, of starving children, kwashiarkor, Oxfam photographs to wring the heart, blindness and brain damage, the world was fed. And with its own choice of cereals; wheat, rice, maize, sorghum, the lot, its own choice of roots, pulses, fruit and green leaves and all free. Packages for children had been devised, mostly by Zeenat Jonsen; it cost little to add the special picture wrapping. Several were tried out to see which appealed most, for example, to South Indian mothers. In a matter of a year baby xeropthalmiah was wiped out. 'You should be very happy, Edmund,' said Marie-Claire after the meeting at which this was announced.

'I am, my dear, I am' he said, and it was very clear that he was. Simply. Without afterthoughts. Without even considering the shareholders. Almost a new experience.

As the Freefood came in some governments started with coupons. But why? Simpler to let people just come and fill their baskets. Sure, there had been hoarding at first, over-buying. The uneducated seemed to think, not without a kind of reason, that the whole thing was a piece of politics, designed by the top people to have an effect on the bottom ones, they did not yet know what. So let us all hurry to fill all our pots, baskets, chests, let us make holes in the ground and bury this food, for it may stop as suddenly as it came! But it

61

did not stop. So, in a little time the new patterns began to emerge, and quite soon it was all taken for granted. Like the free breathable atmosphere of earth.

# CHAPTER NINE

In spite of everything said or done by both sides, there was still no major war. From the Board's point of view there was nothing to be gained by war. They were not into armaments, or only very marginally. It would have been bad for their image. Besides, even a small war was inconvenient and disrupting. It was not too difficult to arrange suitable economic and political pressures on the various national armament industries. Swords could profitably be turned into ploughshares or, more usually, into space-racing. It appeared that there was a generally stabilizing feeling about, although prices of anything beyond the unprocessed Freefood took some years to steady, for it soon became plain that food preparation had to be paid for. Meat eaters did not save so much as those who had lived on cheaper crops, but all the same, when the whole cost of growing fodder was taken off, prices dropped. Devout Hindus no longer had to be worried (if they ever were) by the sight of half-starved bulls. And there was milk and ghee for all, a deliberate part of PAX policy in certain parts of the developing world, even though it meant some extra labour and simple processing. Sea fish were still dear because most of them are the end of a long food chain. But the vegetable-eating freshwater fish which are so important in some cultures could be easily fed, caught and processed. For most of the Western world what this meant was that old-fashioned fish fingers had become a luxury, something for grand-parents to talk about nostalgically.

Early on the Board had considered very carefully whether the care and immediate harvesting of the various crops should be their responsibility and decided that, as a simple matter of control and the avoidance of local profiteering and corruption, they had to be. The same with primary transport, always the difficulty up to now as the many aid organizations working on famines had found to their cost. It had been curiously difficult to get all this across to every member of the Board. Ruiz for example had objected to what he considered gross overpayment to field workers who, he considered again, were no better than peasants. Peons! Sir Edmund shook his head regretfully. How sad if Ruiz could not see the quite obvious long term benefit to PAX! Not to speak of the image improvement.

Gradually the world became so used to PAX products and methods that none of them were any longer newsworthy, or only after the media had been stimulated by something from Ideas. The direct impact was of course much less in the developed world. Processing and marketing Western-style are not cheap. People could still spend the equivalent of a month's wages for a smart dinner. Just as real diamonds were still worth making an effort for, that is if you like diamonds. But even in the developed world basic prices were down, including bread, milk and beer, though the wine growers had successfully resisted experimental work on the chateaux grapes. Tea and coffee were not included in

Freefood and were only slightly down in price since now that the pickers did not come to work in the plantations through sheer hunger, wages had to go up. There had been some European distribution of almost free flour, oatmeal and maize products, but the demand was not great; people prefer their favourite package. But a steady equalization was now going on between developed and underdeveloped countries. Indian and African children grew statistically several inches and gained several kilos in weight. Their IQs rose correspondingly and also consequently their expected standards of dress, housing, amusement, sport and even education. Women began to demand, and even to get, piped water for their houses. More flowers were grown.

Yes, it was highly gratifying to watch how the saddening statistics of world health had changed, still more for those on tour to see the new look of the Indian subcontinent or many an African and South American State. Clothing, especially for the poorer cotton wearing areas, became vastly cheaper. There was even some free distribution of basic undyed cloth. The curse of Adam was gone. Those who had toiled day after day in hope of a harvest which would carry them to another year saw their dream fulfilled. In India many banias were ruined. People no longer mortgaged their rice crop for today's food. Yet social patterns could not change at once among the peoples who had been doing the same things for centuries or longer. They took the Freefood, but still worried about ploughing their own rice fields or planting their own yams. What were the women to do if they did not go to their gardens? They might get into mischief. It was bad enough in the old days of colonial rule when the men had to discover some occupation other than fighting, but at least they had been able to occupy themselves with politics. Unluckily that kind of politics was mostly about themselves as deprived, oppressed and starved, and some of the impetus had been taken out of that.

So there were still problems. How much interest our lives would lose without problems! Saranjit's elder son Harnam found that some of these problems and their solutions made excellent material for films. He was now working mainly for PAX in the really fascinating Ideas section where the image was constantly being remade, improved and adapted, possibly thought to be too obvious, perhaps used to convey a health or peace message. Great care was taken over this. It was a multinational outfit; one day Harnam came home from a working conference with an American-style haircut. Saranjit was angry but Nandu stopped him from saying too much. The thing was done. The boy seemed at least to have kept his bracelet. Perhaps that was a Western fashion! They had known for some time that the alcohol consumption in Ideas was high and it had been quite impossible, Harnam said, to be an abstainer. Why, everyone would have laughed! And that would have been bad for the Sikh image. He might almost have lost his promotion and that would never have done, would it?

Fortunately the younger brother Rahul was still completely a Sikh as well as developing as a scientist. He was quieter; when he was talking taxonomy he was almost boringly willing to go on and on, but was that perhaps hiding something deeper? Anne, who was very fond of him – as he was of her – thought so. In fact he sometimes managed to make himself clear to her about something he was thinking and wondering about, rather than to his father. But Saranjit himself was beginning to suffer from fits of depression, luckily never so far for very long. But why did they come? What was making them?

However, short hair or long, the Ideas section of PAX had

plenty to do. Just as well from the employment point of view. It became clear that PAX was moving in sometimes unexpected directions. There had been a dramatic take-over of one of the main tobacco companies but the Board, in spite of genuine surprise from a few members, refused to think in terms of free cigarettes or pipe tobacco. They cut down on overseas advertising and pressure and tended to encourage smallholders who were still interested in crop production – including cloves for east Asian cigarettes – and who had a suitable climate, to grow their own. Opium production was a still more complex problem and by no means settled yet. Just over a year ago two quite high-powered and sensible PAX agents had mysteriously disappeared in the poppy-growing area of the far Eastern highlands. In spite of protests and even threats, nothing had been made clear. There had not even been a formal apology, still less a return either of the agents or their corpses. The issue was on the verge, between government diplomacy which could be arranged and a show of force which might unhappily escalate, and PAX was especially anxious to keep out of this.

Fortunately other possible sources of friction had smoothed themselves out. The Japanese top-country urge had petered out; some Japanese citizens did not even work or bother to look as if they were working. Instead there were high quality poetry readings. There had been an attempt by the big industrialist-politicians to stop Freefood for deliberate non-workers, but a tactful meeting with the Board had finished that. The practice of magic was to count as work, and indeed it is often as exhausting as coal mining. Relations with the Soviet Union were quite good, and, as they became less alarmed about the intentions of the rest of the world, policies became increasingly relaxed and considerable degrees of freedom emerged. PAX brought in the Freefood, using their own carriers and control methods but not worried about brand names and such. If people supposed it was all done by the Politburo it did not really matter. And there had been some worthwhile meetings between members of research stations. Anne had really enjoyed herself on a trip across the Arctic Circle, came back looking better than she'd done for years. They gave her a fur coat which Marie-Claire said, if remodelled, would be marvellous, but completely! 'It is the very finest natural sable,' Marie-Claire went on, stroking it. 'Only millionairesses have such coats. Or the grandes cocottes in the old days before all this amateurism. Will you let me take it and have it re-designed for you, cherie?'

'But when would I wear it?' said Anne.

'We shall have a special board meeting in Alaska, I think, and invite you!'

In fact there was a special board meeting soon afterwards, though not in Alaska, but for a very exciting announcement. Sir Edmund and most of his fellow members felt that the Peace Prize was deserved. Anne and Saranjit had the Feltrinelli – it hadn't been the Nobel because there had been the obvious claim from the immunology crowd that year and morphogenisis was not the in-science. Besides, from the Nobel Committee's point of view, it was the development that counted, the effect on people. All the Board members within quick plane reach had come. But Ruiz had been assassinated only a few weeks earlier. There were groups in most countries who insisted on misunderstanding what PAX was all about in spite of the films and radio or newspaper publicity, in spite of the best efforts of Ideas. But they were small groups; the larger countries were keeping quiet.

Some Board members were looking, quite simply,

delighted. But others were wondering was it possible that what they had been doing for such a variety of reasons mostly connected with money could have this effect? To stop war? Something which had always been happening? But Sir Edmund was on his feet: 'Over the centuries, indeed the millenia,' he said, 'wars have been fought for territory and what was the territory for? We all know. Food, ladies and gentlemen, food. Now – perhaps that is over. Let me read you the telegram.'

Ethel Gabani had burst into tears. As a child she had known what it was to go without food. And then after many years to become Minister of Health in her little island country, but always to be frustrated because children were still going hungry. And then to be invited to join the PAX Board, although she hardly ever said a word. It was only now in the last few years that it had dawned on her that at last she could be proud and happy with her job, since at last health had become a possibility. Alberto sat back and purred, he had half known this was coming: his sources . . . Professor Ferguson hoped his sister-in-law would read about it in the papers. But would the *Arbroath Advertiser* carry it? Was it as important as the church outing? It would be in the *Scotsman* right enough, but did she ever read anything but the letters and that mostly to disagree with them? Ah, well. Lady Martin nodded vigorously, blew her nose, coloured a little. They were all happy she had been there; she died later that summer, quite quietly, travelling first class in an Inter-City train, the Guardian on her lap. What could be nicer?

Marie-Claire caught Sir Edmund's eye and nodded. The Peace Prize. This would look well, but how long would it last? People seem always to find something to fight about, industrial power, psychological power. But power for what?

Logically for food, the means of life. But, most fortunately people are not logical.

For a time it seemed governments were adjusting. So were the politicians who had spoken so often in terms of the hungry masses. If the balance could be kept everything might go on nicely. But PAX was not idle. There were other needs, as the Board knew very well and had expanded into early on. In addition they had been careful and not always strictly in the public eye when picking up this and that during the chaotic period when the food markets, especially wheat, began to topple; the Big Seven who had controlled the grain market for so long, had, most conveniently, fallen out with one another. At one time there had been this idea, that if people were satisfied over their daily bread there might be a certain sluggishness elsewhere, but instead the pressure of other felt needs rose. There were more consumers, so many millions more that a much smaller profit margin made sense. Needs could be stimulated if necessary; PAX could deal with that quite easily, just a word to Ideas.

Apart from all that, there had been some interesting and not always expected results from the Freefood programme. Some could be seen. At first the birthrate, as well as the survival rate, had gone up, but after a few years it settled, then dropped. People could now afford other relaxations and other insurance against a hungry old age, and at last it became possible to plan for a static world population.

Naturally these new consumers had to find the money for their new needs, the amusements, the gadgets, the elaborations of life, not to speak of housing and education. Secondary industries did well, but still there was worrying unemployment in a few countries, enough to keep the Board busy. Perhaps every social change has its drawbacks. So far

69

most of history is about just that. Some classes of people had been pulled right down, including the old-fashioned farmers of all countries. So it was no surprise to the Board that there was now a fairly respectable anti-morphogenesis movement gathering up all sorts of allies, especially after the bad patch in which, after an attempt to build in on a known vitamin deficiency, the model turned out to have produced semi-lethal alkaloids of a kind which had never so far occurred in nature, and which were not spotted in time. However, most of the casualties were in a rather remote part of South America.

# CHAPTER TEN

Neil Ritchie looked out over miles and miles of wheat, stretching away beyond where he could see, in what had once been flat desert. But at one side it was being cut: one enormous harvester on the ears, another machine behind burying the stalks since the soil needed everything one could get into it. That was why this wheat was designed with so much leafage. It was all very well getting N with the new methods, but P and K had to come from somewhere and desert soil wears out. However, he was thinking now of what more could be got reasonably simply out of the same old sea. Yet another humming and clanking machine was picking up the huge corn bags, the mechanical arms taking them easily, no longer the hard labour of mens' arms. Neil tilted his hat further over his eyes, for the January sun was hot and the wheat glittered, its out-size ears standing erectly golden. Further off still he could hear the humming of more great harvesters. His doing, he supposed. But what would come of it? He was considering the slight problem of Judith-Ann, not that it was any of his business. She had got herself laid. Well, that was to be expected and likely as not by Mike or even Fred for a start. Or the Monash bloke. She used to go to these parties, always ended the same way, all over the floor. I could have had her easy, he thought. That time she came in close and wearing next to nothing, the silly bitch, when I was working, and put her arms round my neck. I told her off. Maybe I'm old-fashioned but it doesn't do in a lab, no, it doesn't do. And then she gets done by this quarter Abo who is working on the feed pumps. Handsome, yes, might be a Greek. Or something. Don't blame her, not a bit. But she wouldn't have an abortion, he couldn't think why, so she has this kid and clear he takes a bit after his great-grandfather. Though why bother nowadays? Her people were furious of course, blamed me. Hadn't wanted her to work with me after she got her degree.

And she'd been good at her job. Reasonably good, that is. Still is for that matter, nothing to complain of. Kid goes to nursery school. Why fuss? He chewed at a wheat ear and wondered what made him go on bothering. Mike, who was angry about it, went and tore up her photo in front of everyone, silly clot. Ah, the hell with the lot of them. He tilted his hat right over his face and slid down onto his back; sweat tickled him. Instead of Judith-Ann, equations began to shape themselves behind his shut eyes as images come for a painter, words for a poet. They were about the input and output of energy or rather of several kinds of energy, working across one another. They were interrupted. He pushed his hat to one side: 'Hello, there. What the hell. Ah, it's you.' Bloke they called Billy-boy. But not his real name.

The dark, handsome, man standing over him grinned in an embarrassed way. 'Yes, me. Sorry.' He was staring at the great golden expanse of wheat. 'That corn, that's all yours.'

'No,' said Neil. 'You've got it wrong, mate. Like you always do. That's PAX corn. They paid for it, all of it. They'll get it. Not me.' He spat out the half chewed corn.

'But it was you, the puzzle reader. You the way maker. You working. We watched you.'

'And so?'

'We want to know what will happen. Who gets it truly? What people? They ask because I work here. I can never say.'

'I've told you till I'm sick tired, Billy-boy. It's to be free food. Bread. For everyone. All Australia, if you understand that much. I know what you're going to say: once it was your people's land. What did they do with it? Walked over it!'

'It gave food then. Not so much. Not for others. But enough for us first Australians.'

'Look, mate, you've got your history wrong. This was desert, sand desert, hot as hell. Couldn't grow food. No way.'

'Far back I'm thinking of. Before the desert.'

'I can't answer for the last glaciation. Nor can you. So come off it.'

The man still stood there, fingers ploughing through wavy black hair. He spoke more softly, deferentially almost. 'About Judith-Ann,' he said.

'Ah, get to hell!' Neil snapped at him.

'That's just where I am, I think sometimes. Hell. Me, burning there. Her people – they hate me. Though I am, yes, I am their grandson's father!'

'Those old fools.' Neil got back reluctantly into the talk, the hum of the harvester was coming nearer, bloody great thing. 'She should have got rid of it.'

72

'She didn't want. She is too brave. But that little boy, he is half me. My people. And she is not.'

Neil stood up, looked at him in anger but also in some sympathy. 'Won't marry you, eh? Just wants the kid for herself. Too bad, mate, but that's how it is these days. You should have thought of that.'

'I did not know. Then – with her – It only seemed – ah, real beaut!'

Yes, thought Neil, that's how the cookie crumbles. Always. For all of us. Like me making this corn. Working at it. Like working up a woman. And what's going to happen? What's this Freefood going to do to the world? Didn't think about it, did we? Too bloody clever. And this poor devil and his problem, why's he got to come to me? People think because we scientists are good at one kind of thing we ought to be good at everything. At consequences. We're not.

Billy-boy was still moaning away: 'I would have worked for her. Made her a home. Me, I don't drink. I have savings. Yes, savings. Dollars in a bank account.'

'And she's not interested. Too bad, mate, Still, she might get bored with the kid, who knows.' He took the man firmly by the arm. 'Here, step back, cobber, we don't want to get in the way of the harvester. Anyway I don't.'

They watched it coming towards them, a big thing, powerful, efficient, but not in any sense beautiful as the wheat was, standing there. 'The corn does not know,' said the man. Looking at it and one another, a thought passed.

'Ah, come off it, mate! It's not thinking. Not feeling. It's there to make bread. Free bread.' The harvester went thundering by, the wheat lay crushed and headless.

'Up north,' said the man, 'my people say no to free food.'

'That Arnhem Land crowd?' said Neil. 'More fools they. But

why? Don't go looking so scared, mate. Just you explain.'

'They say because – because it is not done with respect. Food is our life, we should respect it. All kinds food. Plants. Animals. Given away it is nothing. We should grow it. Hunt it. Fish it out of water. Know its inside. And what else should a man do? Or a woman? In Arnhem Land, that is Murngin, they say they only want food if – if it is worked for. Respected. Spoken to. Put into pictures.'

'I worked for this,' said Neil. 'I made kind of pictures. Graphs. Equations, pretty equations.'

The man half understood. 'Yes but – you did not become part of it.'

'How do you know?'

'So. Perhaps you did. Maybe I get you wrong, Boss. So maybe true you joined up with the corn. The water. All that new water. But then came the big harvesters. Not understanding, not joining up, them. And few people.' He pointed at the machine and shook his head and looked at Neil with those dark sad eyes, and for a moment Neil knew how that silly bitch Judith-Ann had fallen for him. The man spoke again. 'The feed pumps. Maybe soon they will work for themselves. Not needing man. Not needing me.'

'We'll find you another job,' said Neil shortly. But this unemployment thing was awkward right enough, though none of his business. Well, it didn't matter if a man was laid off; he could still eat. Or perhaps it did matter. Not to be able to use one's skills. He wouldn't like to be laid off himself. Not that he ever would be. Ah, that would bugger up a good few things! And that lot of Abos up north playing around with their own land that they could do what they liked with, a state inside a state. Turning white men off, so he'd heard, and a good thing too most likely. The white Australians had given the land back with both hands

74

because of their bad conscience. And why not? His own grand-parents had come out after that first lot had stopped murdering the Abos, so he had no guilt of his own. Or not much. But what were they up to not wanting his bread corn? One day, he thought, I'll find that out. 'If you lost your job here,' Neil asked, 'would you want to go to Arnhem Land?' After a moment the man nodded. 'You – mostly white?'

'The other side of me would – would take my feet. Up north,' he whispered to Murngin. Then looked straight at Neil: 'But – with my son.'

'I see' said Neil quite gently. 'So I'm afraid it's off.' And I'd better warn Judith-Ann he thought, just in case. But the man drooped, no, he'd never do anything violent, probably wouldn't even try to go north all that way to Arnhem Land. Or would he?

# CHAPTER ELEVEN

Rahul Singh was watching the back of the pilot. He was in a very small, old fashioned plane, almost within touch of all the passengers. The two at the front, by the quite small bank of switches and clock faces were, he decided, both young women. Though it is always difficult to be certain in another culture. He was the only Caucasian in the plane, the only light brown, though one other passenger, a thin elderly woman must, he thought, be a half or quarter caste; he had begun to realize that there had been a considerable gathering-in, from other parts of

Australia, of those with some aboriginal background, to the almost independent state of Arnhem Land. No, Murngin, he must think of it correctly. Many still kept the brow ridge, not unbecoming as it set off the eyes below, just as an orthodox Moslem's woman's nose-veil sets off her eyes above.

He felt strangely alien. They were mostly speaking in English, but of a kind he found hard to follow, used as he was by now to the Australian accent. This was different again. Sometimes there were phrases in another language, totally unintelligible, but usually laughter-provoking. The man in the seat next to him was wearing a standard short-sleeved cotton shirt, but just above the elbow elaborately woven arm-bands with feathers threaded through them. One of those in front had feathers in some way secured to his hair, which had the usual brilliant black wave, so different from the Melanesian fuzz in the last two islands where he had been bringing the systematic botany up to date. He still found it difficult to tell one of the Australian aboriginals from another; a face would seem vaguely familiar, but could he be certain? He somehow felt he had seen the man with the arm-bands before, but perhaps only in an illustration in some book, for he had been doing a good deal of reading up even though he distrusted the written word, preferring his own observations.

It was alien country too. They had been skirting mud flats where the slow rivers wound down to the sea, which shallowed so gradually that you could not be sure, from the plane, where land ended and water began. Nor yet which were salt inlets burrowing inland among mangroves and crocodiles. The loops and bends of the rivers gradually worked down along the current, through the soft soil, pushing a few feet of mud every year until at last the warm tides submerged them. An interesting flora, but he could have done without some of the fauna. He bent to examine the bites and stings on his legs. Well, that was to be expected. At the same time he noticed curious scars on the legs of the man next to him, probably made deliberately for some purpose he could not guess. Or could he? Odd to get so close to a quite other kind of – religion, wasn't it? – but to have so little idea what it was about, except that it was deeply to do with places and what had, or might have, happened there.

And yet: there had been that earlier visit. He had so nearly forgotten it. One is a different person at fourteen to oneself at the end of education, almost twenty-four years old. He remembered being with Anne Tomlin, their talks, the way she had shown him little matters of observation which he might have brushed over. He had forgotten what else he had seen and heard and absorbed. Or had he? He thought back as hard as he could. The feathered arm-bands? Had he seen this before on someone – or in a dream? One must be completely objective, not trust to dreams. But – were they dreams? The anthropology books used this phrase 'the dreaming' for the aboriginal past, for the cultural build up. And now he remembered the water hole and the man he thought he had seen, and afterwards Anne opening a tin of chicken. If he listened hard perhaps he might come across a word or two which he had known or half known in those old days. He tried to switch into a different kind of attention.

They had turned inland now; he could see the old scarrings of opencast mining –bauxite, uranium? – but that was all finished. Yet if people refused the Freefood and also cut off their main source of revenue, mining royalties, what were they living on? Here, higher up, it looked like barren empty land, dried and brown, near desert, though sometimes there was jungle of some kind; 'bush' the Australians said. So funny! Here and there were green acres of cultivation, mostly along river valleys, as well as other human evidence. But oh, how much emptier than the crowded largeness of India! And there – he tried to make out through the small window – was this hydroelectric power? Irrigation? Did they have that? Well, he would see.

The plane began to dip towards the small settlement which he had selected as his centre when he had asked leave from the Northern Council to come in and look for plants, not, he explained, to exploit them in any way, nor to take out more than a few specimens, only what he could carry with him. All he wanted was to put them into their own honourable place in a great scheme of things called botanical taxonomy. He had been stopped at the road block east of Darwin; people had met him there and looked through his pass and asked him questions, all quite amiably.

He was beginning to see the vegetation now. Clearly the high plateau could grow little and might be very cold in winter. But as they slid past the cliffs there were all the expected eucalyptus species but also cypresses, and a mix of probably deciduous trees, and between them thick growths of cycads and screw-palms. And what would there be below? It had never been properly covered. He couldn't wait!

Now they were fastening seat-belts and the plane's wheels extended. He was watching the girl pilot handling the controls with no bother, even rather casually, and found he was suddenly engulfed in unease, surprize and definite fear, then felt ashamed of himself. Clearly these girls knew what they were doing. Oh, he must write about it to Anne! She would understand, would forgive the bad moment. The great Anne Tomlin. Then all at once something else flicked into his mind: the man next to him with the armlets, who had been looking through a two-day-old copy of *The Australian* and occasionally turning back to the man in the seat behind with some remark about it, usually in accented English – and Aussie English was hard enough to follow! – was the same who had questioned him at the road block. And possibly the same as the man he had seen on his first trip, sitting carelessly in the dust among the deserted and ugly mine buildings at Gove, writing notes on a small pad.

The plane came to a halt. Rahul got out and stretched. The pilot leaned over the door and spoke to the man with the armbands. Yes, there was a word of greeting which he rememberd! Both looked round at Rahul, who wondered what was happening, could not read their faces. Were they angry? Was it possible that he was in some way – trapped? If he had been marked and followed, for what? He had not much liked his short visit to Neil Ritchie who had snapped at him as though he somehow blamed Saranjit and Anne for – again, what? But now he almost wished he was back in South Australia. No, no, what would Anne say, even his father! A Sikh does not fear.

The girl pilot in her white overalls climbed out of the plane and came up to him solemnly; what was she going to say? He made a dab at the greeting word, got it partly wrong, but it seemed she understood, for slowly her face broke into a wide smile, enormously reassuring: 'Djiuvalji says you come to look for plants. Right?'

'Yes,' he said, 'yes, that is so.'

'But also he says you may come from Freefood people. You were in the south with Ritchie.'

'Yes,' he said, 'but why worry? I am not part of his outfit'.

'You come from India. Where the thing started. Ritchie knew you. But you have to understand: we do not want the Freefood from him. Our people there saw you speak with him, some times.'

'He told me you didn't want it. Perhaps some day you might like to change your minds; people do that. But I have not come here to ask you to take it. No!'

'That is good then. But I think still you do not understand.

79

Maybe you will – later.'

Now the man with the arm-bands spoke: 'Why you come here? Small place, this. Why not Oenpelli?'

'Oenpelli is too big. Too many houses. Too many people. They walk on the plants.'

The two who were questioning him and the others who were listening all laughed – 'Oenpelli too big! Right!' The girl laughed too, her black curls bouncing, spoke over her shoulder to her co-pilot who was still in the cabin, then said: 'Right! Djiuvalji will show you the house for strangers.' And then added, but why? 'Djiuvalji is not my cousin.'

'Shall I see you again?' Rahul asked quickly, but she only smiled and went back to the plane. She was a nice girl, but totally unattractive, at least to him. But there was something very strange, very curious. Part of the Australian curiousness, the banksias, the dicksonias, all the myrtaceae just a bit different, the black-boys growing with millenial slowness, or flowers that had designed themselves only to be fertilized by tiny beetles, or enormous, ungainly moths, as the beetles and moths, co-existing, had designed themselves for the flowers. And these people who refused the Freefood, was it to put pressure on someone or something? But they had got what they wanted from Australia, it was not Gandhi's salt-march. He just didn't know where to start thinking, and watched her start the plane and taxi off.

The man with the arm-bands spoke quietly: 'Come! No use looking for that plane. Narbudja has taken it away. You are with us. We give you bed. We give you food. Not Freefood!' and he burst out laughing, but then, more seriously: 'No beer. No wine. We do not drink here. Nor our guests.'

'I have never in my life touched alcohol,' said Rahul Singh, looking straight at the other man and remembering how some of Ritchie's outfit had teased him for just this. And he, being a Sikh, had stuck to it.

'Good,' said Djiuvalji.

# CHAPTER TWELVE

Anne seemed to go from worry to worry. The South American alkaloid deaths had upset her terribly. She ought to have done more tests, ought perhaps to have foreseen the possibility of something of this kind going wrong, if not one way, then some other way. There were papers she hadn't read. There were ideas going round that she hadn't properly taken in. Sometimes a paper or a report would be worthless except for one sentence which one would have to spot – to encourage and make grow like a seedling. But one can't be everywhere and the Centre had got so big; even walking round could be tiring. And there was this new breathlessness and sometimes cramp – was it cramp, or the rheumatism that the ageing can expect? – over the chest area and down her arms. She supposed she ought to see a doctor, but what a bore doctors always are, always wanting to make changes either in one's metabolism or one's habits.

She was a little upset to find Saranjit not as worried as she was about the undiscovered alkaloids. But he was in one of those fits of depression to which he was becoming increasingly subject. Depressions did not fit his make-up. His wife, still lovely Nandu, asked Anne's advice and tried everything, including quite remarkable feats both of cookery and of sex. But no. There is no reason for these things except that we are all dependent on the incredibly fine adjustments in our internal chemistry going just right. And these in turn may be partly dependent on feelings, outlook, anxieties, doubts, call it what you will. Yet in the old days Saranjit had not been bothered this way; all would be sublimated in action.

Could it be that what Anne and Saranjit and their immediate team were doing now was less exciting, did not, as it was expressed once, stir the blood? They were filling gaps, occasionally coming up with some new notion, watching how something developed, having long technical arguments, titivating a piece of apparatus or a way of thinking. But in the main they were allowing or assisting others to go ahead over whatever was being suggested by the Board's planning and nutrition experts, sometimes rationalizing food production as an old but labour-intensive crop dropped out of fashion, sometimes making interesting additions, usually designed to raise the health level somewhere. Zeenat buzzing around, leaving her trail of scent! But more was in the hands of the programmers and the computer section, storing and using and discarding information. Must research always end like this?

The American NIF crowd seemed to have got their noses down to some new possibilities, but were being distinctly cagey: a pity but understandable. No papers of any consequence had been coming out, only an occasional rumour. Neil Ritchie wrote cross postcards, often mildly obscene; he must have taken some trouble getting hold of them. All irritatingly heterosexual too: those Australians! And he doesn't seem to have been nice to dear Rahul, thought Anne gloomily.

If the members of the Board came to visit, Saranjit became, Anne thought critically, more Indian than he used to be, the Head of the Department, the senior Guru, the Weaver of impossible theories, the Deflector of awkward questions. It was all on the outside, a defence mechanism; inside, the depression went on. It was only Alberto who ever got through to him at all. They swapped silly schoolboy jokes, but at least it was on a human level. No doubt there was a deliberate cut-off.

And she herself? She cut off as well, though differently. Cut off from Sir Edmund, however good his manners and even his intentions. Cut off from Dr. Schulman and Prof Ferguson, even when they had sensible and relevant questions. Anne was, quite simply and understandably, not to be found when Board members came to visit the Centre. Or she was in the critical middle of a piece of work, not to be disturbed and she had no qualms about telling little protective lies. She felt they had taken something from her which she valued, though she could not quite tell what. Her F.R.S. was somehow tarnished. By them. Her worth, her dignity as a scientist, where had it gone? Perhaps it didn't matter. Or was it the same thing which was getting at Saranjit? The Board. Them.

But a visit from Marie-Claire was different, oh how different! She had just flown in, landing at the charming little air-strip where the first breath a passenger took on disembarking was full of the scent of deep forest, of growth, of the greening of countless leaves. For a moment Marie-Claire stood on the step, breathing deeply and feeling herself becoming taller and more correctly balanced with the kind of muscular and respiratory response which she had felt in the old days at the opening bars of the on-stage invitation. No, what she felt now was simply the thought of Anne, her darling: to be with her, to touch her. There was this little thing to be said, but it didn't matter. Nothing mattered: heaven. Yes, there was Anne as she had known she would be.

For of course Anne had gone to meet her happily, pushing

away a set of figures which could wait. She was going to ask Marie-Claire to suggest a competent doctor whom she could consult about her mild but annoying aches and pains. Marie was always so clear about marginals like money and doctors and which of the things the Board fussed about needed to be attended to, so much cleverer than she herself was! But somehow Anne, while they looked and greeted and took one another in again, let it slip. How curiously pleasant it was just to be with Marie again, to bring her home, to rest together during the heat, watching the whir of the great ceiling fans which Anne, unlike Saranjit and Nandu, so much preferred to air-conditioning. There they were together in the welcoming room open to them with music, books, pictures, cushions, to talk, to touch, ah to enjoy, to send the blood racing back into the dry channels, to wake all those tingles of tension which had been asleep, then to collapse into mutual, delicious laughing otherness and easing of all tensions; peace.

And after that there would be cool showers and tea would be brought to the verandah among the flowers: tea fragrantly steaming with fresh sliced limes, and in the little silver filigree dishes which had once belonged to Anne's grandfather, nuts and small spicy delicacies or halved mangoes, dripping for licked fingers. And sinking into the deep happiness and comfort of both being once more in the same place, the same piece of history and the same sweet affection. 'I know I shall get the best tea in the world with you, my Anne' said Marie-Claire sipping.

'It was an early improvement, you know, Marie, never bettered. But it isn't the most popular!'

Marie-Claire was not as happy as she might have been, because dear Anne was looking somehow a little more tired than usual. Those curiously drawn lines round her eyes and mouth seemed to have gone deeper. Yes, they could be eased for a small space in delight, then sadly reasserted themselves. Her Anne who was so enormously superior, not only in understanding but in this selfless research, this seeking down past what ordinary people could understand! – Anne Tomlin not interested in trivial feelings or possessions, not ever caring about her own dear self. So what was it? It must be the question which was bothering them both, yet not so easy to put one's finger onto it. Oh not so easy at all.

Relaxed and refreshed, Marie tried to put it into exact words in her own mind, choreographed, made to stay or move. Yes, she had it. There should have been an increase of human happiness in the well-fed world, and it should have been measurable. In fact the media, full of those stupid, arrogant men of ideas, thought they'd got it by the short hairs, but the real proofs of happiness simply did not exist. Anne knew that. Certainly there was an absence of acute misery of one kind, but is that enough for man in God's image, that phrase to which dear Sir Edmund is so boringly addicted? People who had once been content if the rice bowl was full now wanted more and again more of everything. As could have been foreseen: as had certainly been foreseen by the Chairman and some of the Board. For a little while those who had been hungry had lain back happily, not working nor stimulated by civilized desires; but television had triumphed, universal video, exciting pictures, live stories of another kind of life, endlessly encouraging people to want to go on wanting, to expect to buy, to go on buying. So now most of them in all continents went at the correct hour, seeing that all now had watches, to their factories or offices where they worked, not necessarily very fast or efficiently and certainly not in bad conditions, but producing and producing, so that, when they came out after not too arduous a day, they could buy and buy. Naturally PAX smiled down on them. But was it all for the best?

'Anne, my sweet,' said Marie-Claire, 'you are disappointed? Seeing that we are not quite living in the Garden of Eden?' She looked round: 'But you at least, is there anything you need? Oh tell me! How I wish, cherie, that you could have brought yourself to accept the shares we offered you at the beginning. You know, the offer could be interpreted as being still open.' For, if Anne could, so to speak, build herself up a little more, perhaps through her immediate environment? One or two good pictures might help. And a really good picture costs money. And rightly. Wine? No, she quite liked an occasional glass, but was totally unable to appreciate a supreme hock. Or a modern space-racing set with all the exciting new music and all the visuals? But no, no, she wouldn't bother to switch on, she'd stick to her old pick-up. Bless her.

But Anne answered: 'That's not what I want.'

'You want to see everyone fulfilled. Not by food. By living – happily, creatively. And that's not happening. At least not everywhere. But certainly we have changed the face of India. And a whole list of other countries. Paraguay, Salvador, Nicaragua, Bolivia, even Brazil, Chad, Mali, Transkei, Campuchea, oh, everywhere. Is that not something good?'

'India' said Anne obstinately, 'is less beautiful.'

'Ah,' said Marie-Claire, 'there are fewer women in saris washing at dirty tanks, fewer naked children, fewer men driving back the oxen in the dust of the evening, those half-starved village oxen! The temples swarming with worshippers, asking, asking, bringing their poor little offerings, their garlands and cracked saucers of this and that, their coloured powders! You cannot really want that back.'

'Each group had some unique quality' Anne said slowly, frowning.

'Ah, that's caste division – cruel!'

'Yes, but the alternative is boring – the same lunch box wherever you go. I'm afraid – yes, love – that we are getting very near a boring society. And I won't be bored!'

'There are worse things. Come, cherie, you know it. War. Hunger.'

'Yes, yes, we can't have that back. But bored people can get very nasty to one another. And look what we have: millions of men and women not knowing what to do next. Not having even the small happiness of thinking of something to make. They used to make all sorts of things in the villages, out of anything they could lay hands on. Now they don't have to do that, and there is a loss. You know that as well as I do!'

'They make all sorts of things still – pretty, local things. And in decent conditions at last. We have gone on supporting village industries. Haven't we had this up at the Board – oh, so often!'

'Yes, yes, I know all that, of course you've played the village industries game – no, don't make that face, love! – but people don't really want to play it themselves. They want the exciting factory things you bring in, consumer goods. Their own hand-made whatsits are devalued. Just as I feel devalued myself – sometimes. The colour going out of the villages – the satisfaction going out of research.' She got up and no, she didn't want Marie, she went over to the bookshelf looking for a special line she wanted in that battered old Shakespeare of hers. He knew all right!

A tear plopped down on to the book. Oh, but Marie couldn't bear it! She tiptoed over, touched, slid her arm round and there was Anne's head cradled for a moment until she looked up, shook herself and then said stormily: 'Spoiling things! Inventing wants! And when we warned them –' she stopped abruptly.

Marie smiled. 'Yes, I know, ma Mie, you did warn them. And some of them even believed you. A few in China became anxious

87

perhaps but there it was a necessary bargain very happily and faithfully carried out. We grew most of their food in the country itself, handed over the management and they enjoyed our imports. And naturally it was known what you said in Zimbabwe and for a time the government there were a little cagey. Not all of them naturally.'

'It was all the people who wanted their little bit of land, had killed and died for it so that it and the food it grew had total value – they didn't want to destroy that!'

'But in the end they were sensible. There are other values.'

'Yes. How did you – the Board – know that we had given them advice of any kind.'?'

'Things get round, cherie. We knew it was only a warning. Which could be taken or disregarded. As we take all warnings, don't we? You had the right to give it.' She led Anne gently back to the sofa. She filled their cups again. A delicious steam wafted between them; she felt better. Was it that between two intelligent women there is always human dignity and equality?

She went on lightly. 'Of course some of the Board were not amused. They're normally stupid and they thought that their other intentions, the follow-up of Freefood, the import of all those nice things people feel they should have now, had been blocked in Zimbabwe or at least might have been interrupted. Remember, cherie, it is not totally cheap to produce the Freefood. Many people are employed and looked after. The Board has to have money to pay for all this.'

'Money!' Anne growled.

'Yes, just that. That silly thing! And only necessary because it simplifies exchange. Now listen! If the Board and the Corporation behind it cannot have the economic benefits which follow the Freefood the whole plan is endangered. It is quite simple, nothing wrong happens. Most people benefit. It is only an exchange process like – like an exchange of gases. So – we have not to upset the balance. You see? And so you could be the tiniest bit – un tout petit peu – more careful, my Anne?'

'Careful!' said Anne. 'I'm not sure I know what *that* means. What you mean it to mean. Or what that Edmund of yours means. That sort of careful. It means very little in basic research which is what I suppose I care about. As for politics – !' She made a little face at Marie Claire.

'I am only asking you to think for a moment for your own sake and also for mine about this little word which I have spoken. Not that there are any suspicions. Oh, no! I think perhaps Edmund is too intelligent for that. But it would be sad – and for the cause of peace – if all the world did not march together for an agreement of some kind about Freefood which should be the same for all. Disagreements, even small ones, may grow. C'est tout, ma douce.' She took a long soft look. Could she have hurt Anne? Oh, not possible. No, Anne's spirit of anger had died down, now she was in another mood. Since love consists of a spectrum of feeling. Love, yes, most certainly. Marie was reaching across for one more nibble at those little spicy biscuits or perhaps the dramatic white and purple of the halved mangosteens, just as Anne was leaning over to fill her cup. And their hands met for a soft moment palm to palm. Marie slid her hand round to cradle the strong muscles in the ball of Anne's thumb while Anne's hand in turn cradled the smoother length from the little finger down wristwards; Marie Claire's hand, so smooth to kiss, to smell, to touch. Touching which is better than words, easier, impossible to misunderstand: touch of the thousand nerve endings in those clever hands we have developed and gentled over the long millenia since our ancestors used them for tree climbing and a little later for throwing stones at one another.

# CHAPTER THIRTEEN

Anne was walking out into the garden with yet more to worry about. For what had Marie-Claire meant by urging her to be careful? In spite of the hand clasp, in spite of the delight in being together again, could it be that Marie was really one of – Them? A destroyer. But did she really think that of the Board? Without whom so much could not have been achieved. Yet, all the same, was it so certain now that she and Saranjit had thought enough about it at the beginning, had foreseen all – but how can one foresee? It is the business of science to foresee, to have made accurate measurements and to deduce from them. But it couldn't be done. They probably said it to history students too! Come, come, you mustn't worry. One must completely disassociate oneself from one's worries. But how? And Marie, who should have helped, had made them worse! What had she meant, what kind of warning? What constraints could the Board put on them? No use asking Saranjit in the mood he was in now.

This was still really her grandfather's garden, just as the big old bungalow somehow remained comfortingly his. The best of the trees had been his planting. But some things were new. There had been a certain amount of work done on the decorative species, especially those, like the orchids, with great plasticity. She doubted whether more than a very few were, in fact, more beautiful than their predecessors. Roses never did well in this climate and she could do without them. She had seen plenty of holograms of the new European rose-inventions, but had not been much impressed. Perhaps she ought to go back to England again, how long was it since she was there last? It would do her good, get her body into trim again. She could, she supposed, see the family again. That was what her grandfather had done; he went home regularly. And, as regularly, came back. There, at the end of the path was one of his little marble summer houses, still standing, unchanged, jasmine ramping over it. He used to worry about keeping people fed. Crop failures. Famines. Well, that was all over. Monsoons might fail now but it didn't matter any longer. There would be a rice harvest somewhere else and nobody would be allowed to turn in into money.

What did matter? Now that everyone could sit back. But they didn't. Instead of the one basic anxiety – our daily bread – they had invented hundreds of new, little ones. It wasn't even as if active, creative world peace had been achieved, in spite of the Nobel and all that. Only that sanctions against war had become more unpleasant. But the big powers still piled up new ways of frightening one another – and themselves. If they didn't, a lot more scientists would be out of their jobs, which presumably they enjoyed in a technical way. She wondered if PAX was into this in spite of their Nobel. Only too probably. But she didn't want to know and above all didn't want to ask Marie. Thank God she hadn't ever been tempted to become a physicist. Instead she had been faithful to the intricate, beautiful world of natural growth. Only was it any longer like that? Now that the ancient patterns of phyllotaxis had been so well understood that they could be partially controlled. But you can't change the mathematics it is all based on. At least – no. But who cares about the patterns of nature? Not the Board. Marie-Claire, did she truly care? Ah, stop worrying about what you cannot alter! Nature will go on doing its things however much or little attention people pay. More of these people live in towns, fewer in direct contact with the natural world. You can't expect them to care. Did that matter? A city is the natural eco-system for modern man. When did she first hear that?

Her hand stroked along a leaf and then another leaf and the cramp she had been feeling only half consciously, eased off.

Cities were not her eco-system. Marie-Claire was perhaps, or had become, a city girl, valuing the delicacies of advanced city life, the cosmetic aspect, the instant communication, the postponement of ageing, at least for some. Yes, that was part of the fun. Marie looked no different now from the first sight they'd had of her on the Board's introductory visit – many years back! But she herself must look different, got more easily tired, found it harder to walk uphill. This was as inevitable as leaf-fall. Without which the natural world would be a duller place. But it was stupid of her not to have asked Marie about a doctor, she had been put off by that – warning. Suddenly she decided she would sit down and write a long letter to Rahul, who like herself did care about the patterns of nature. Where to? Probably care of the Institute, Darwin. That fascinating, subtle, north Australian flora! He'd pick her letter up some time. She turned back towards the bungalow, stone and wood and creepers, the sun-birds always darting among them. A cool drink was quickly and smilingly brought to her.

The letter started off with family and professional news. What did he think about these bad depressions his father got into? She herself thought it could be explained something like this: 'He and I were always socially committed scientists. We felt that it was an inherently moral thing to increase the sum of human knowledge. But physicists might, against their will and often without their knowledge, find that their work was contributing to increasingly horrible methods of warfare. Many years ago I was approached to contribute to some research on defoliation. Naturally it was called Defence! But I wrote back one of those indignant letters that end up in an official waste paper basket.

'Well, then, the time came when your father and I began to realize the possibilities of morphogenesis. We could hardly speak about it at first. But when it became clear that manipulation of the kind we had already managed could produce not only different

92

forms of petal or leaf or bract, but also the basic changes which we know so well now, we were frightened. Frightened and excited, both of us, though your father wouldn't have admitted such a thing as fear! There had been so much spoken and written about the population of earth outrunning their food supplies and we had both seen, in various parts of the world, large groups of people near starvation and in constant anxiety about their next meal, worst perhaps in our own India. So when PAX approached us and we began to have long and increasingly practical discussions, we ended up thinking we were doing the right thing. We consulted various colleagues and there was general agreement on this. You know, the PAX offer meant many more posts, not only on the botanical and micro-biologocal side, but on administration and the computer outfit.

'Well, that's ancient history, but now I go back to it and I wonder, I wonder. There were other workers in our field who would almost certainly have come to the same conclusions. It wasn't really in our hands even if we did make the initial break-through. So now all the world is fed. Some firms, smaller ones, would have acted less honourably on that. Perhaps we ought to have tried harder with the F.A.O., but you know how slow inter-national agencies are, and such a lot of interference and extra bother and getting in an international team who would probably have messed up all our work! At least PAX doesn't suffer from bureaucracy. But all that has been done seems not to have increased the sum of human happiness. Some of it is that people have got so deep into the habit of working for their daily bread that they find it difficult – uncomfortable – not to be doing so. But the other thing is that now they seem to want all sorts of rather stupid possessions and amusements and are unhappy if they don't get them. It's this kind of disappointment with what's gone wrong that gets at me and probably your father as well. He won't

93

admit it to me but he might to you. So when are you coming back, Rahul dear? Why not put through a reversed charge video? It might cheer your father up. And have you found anything exciting?'

She enclosed a photo of one of his sisters, with her very suitable husband and baby boy. But would he answer – ? She hoped so. It had taken a kind of weight off to write to him. But where had he got to? She thought he must be in Arnhem Land, in the closed country that most of the Australians wouldn't mention if they could help it. Undemocratic, they said, and no doubt it was, but that wasn't her own pet ideology. The undemocratic thing the white Australians disliked so much was not allowing drink, but the Aboriginals knew quite well what harm that had done to their own people and were determined to keep it out. Good for them, she thought, and Rahul, being a real Sikh, won't worry. So long as he was all right. They still went in for spears and initiations and all that. But he was a sensible boy.

She began to plan a visit to England, to meet some cousins who, she knew, had kept a good many of her grandfather's letters; she would like to see them, to know more about him. And then, a month later, she got the return letter from Rahul. It was long and carefully sealed over. She read it once quickly, and then a second time, trying to take it in. She saw immediately why he hadn't wanted to have a long distance conversation overheard, as it well might have been, considering the relations between Arnhem Land, or whatever they called it now, and Darwin, the capital of the white northern state. But perhaps the Institute was not bugged. Scientists don't normally like to get involved in this type of political action.

On the first page of the letter he wrote briefly about botanical matters, a small extension of the bounds of knowledge, but that was not what was now, apparently, eating him. He went on to explain that Arnhem Land, but he always called it Murngin, had refused to let in the Freefood – did she know that? But yes, she had heard and thought it curious, as the inhabitants were reckoned to be underfed. But that was by Australian standards. She had supposed that this was a temporary thing; some American and Canadian sects had also refused it to start with, but that hadn't lasted.

However, according to Rahul, who seemed to be taking it completely seriously, these people in Murngin State had some kind of relationship with the land itself which meant a mutual giving and assisting and respecting. Anne was always a bit suspicious when the word 'love' was used, and it came several times into Rahul's letter. He explained that the people of this part of Australia had been hunters, fishers and gatherers, but above all had lived in a continuous eco-system for some fifty thousand years, during which various kinds of understanding had developed with others in the eco-system, both animal and vegetable, and with the earth itself. (And here Anne began to waggle her eyebrows.) There had been no predators, no wolves or lions or such, and so much space that there was no need for aggression towards other human groups. This had been happening instead of technological developments of the kind that are usually thought to be necessary for advanced civilization. They were still fishers and gatherers of wild fruit, nuts, roots and leaves, but many had settled for such crop agriculture as was possible in a rather difficult land. They had kept off the highly destructive cattle and sheep of their white neighbours. And by general agreement they were not allowing the entry of Freefood which, they said, would destroy the relationship between them and their land with its so many gifts and personifications and dreaming.

'There will be pressure put on them to accept the Freefood,' he went on, 'and you can and must stop it, you and my father.

He must pull himself together! You two must say it is an essential experiment, leaving them alone. They are the control group. You can think what to say, but think quick, Anne! There is not so much time. Remember how happy you and I were when I was just a kid and we went off together and boiled our billy of tea and you showed me which berries I could eat? And there was that fungus which you stopped me so hard from eating until you had tried it out yourself! That was relationship with the eco-system. Anne, you would so much love Murngin now. They have made their own laws which have been built up from the earth and the past and they refuse to let anyone else come in permanently. Even the mine managers, the few who are left, on old agreements, can only stay a certain time. The mines stay very strictly within bounds. White miners get the Freefood and sealed crates of beer. But my friends know there are better ways than alcohol of attaining another vision; it is perhaps a little like yoga, only different. It is very funny when you think back to Australian history. But it must go on. It is value for all the world. Anne, you will help them to do it their way? Please! For all these people. And me.'

But oh dear, how could she? A control group? They had never thought of keeping one community out of the great pattern of Freefood. It would have had to be discussed already, probably with the Board. How could she pretend and be believed? She would at least have mentioned it to Marie-Claire. And was this the kind of thing Marie-Claire had been warning her about? Perhaps. And if so – I had better speak to Saranjit. Dear Rahul, he has found systematic botany boring: no doubt it is. And so he has become involved in – in politics. Yes, she was afraid it was that. But, could he have hit on something important?

She re-read his letter. He seemed to be involved with two people, men she supposed, or was Naburdja a woman? He never described them, only named Djiuvalji and Naburdja – she suspected the spelling was only an approximation to the pronunciation – as friends and informants. The common language, he said rather priggishly, was always English, and better than that of many white Australians. She smiled over his comment. His own English had a definite Indian accent, a tip-up at the end of the sentence, especially when he got excited. Perhaps he was getting at Neil Ritchie, who, she remembered, had a fruity Australian accent even if his grand-parents had come from Oban.

And then she looked again at the P.S. in pencil: 'Do you remember when we were here together that man I saw, who disappeared? Now I think I saw true.' But good gracious, that must be nonsense! Rahul of all people going soft on fact – and I hoped he'd forgotten.

But then she tucked this into the back of her mind and began to wonder about the main content of the letter: the relationship between people and environment. Had Rahul hit on some kind of solution to what was worrying her – and others? But was it applicable to any community in, let's say, the developed world? That was something else again and the answer was probably not. And the vanishing man? No, no! Or could this possibly be in some way a universal idea which had gone underground? A hidden river?

# CHAPTER FOURTEEN

The weeks went by. Rahul ticked them off in his calendar which had an old fashioned elephant on the cover.

All along the deep-cut river beds, however dry after months of continuous burning sun, there was still an astonishing variety of plants, as he had suspected there might be. But higher up on the dry plateau, ridged with uncompromisingly rock-piled hills, there seemed to be little but an eternity of spiked spnifex as far as sight could go. Yet here too, there were sometimes hollows and ridges which always meant some kind of change. Rahul, alone in his tent, made notes and drawings and thought about what was puzzling him, and thought about what he would write to Anne. He thought also about the two who had been guiding and answering him.

But many miles away, far out of sight and hearing, Naburdja was in the dance. But here she had another name; much of her was now altogether other. She had left her old light blue jeans which she wore when she was out of uniform, well clear of the dance ground, on a little clump of thorny bushes at the far side of the ridge. For a few minutes, as she crossed the ridge, naked, she felt shy and chilly. But once the paint had been put on her, she knew herself to be properly and sufficiently clothed, as the rest equally did. She adjusted the feathered bands, felt up to her newly tied hair. She watched her breathing beginning to change, becoming first quick and shallow, then deep and heavy: with it her perceptions changed, her body began to become other. Far off, it seemed. The older women, sitting round the fire, shouted formal insults; the younger ones pretended to be frightened. Then, gradually, the dance began as one after the other slipped into it, as one might slip into a deep, swirling pool fed from a vast waterfall. The singing, low and spasmodic at first, gathered strength as music sticks joined in. The stars swung over the gap in the hill. The aroused earth answered the feet, the spread of toes, sometimes the spread of fingers, the beat of knees or elbows as the dancers became now one thing, now another, flying as birds, swimming as fish, crawling as snakes, bounding, climbing, speaking with the voice of animals or of the dead. By the end of the night their dancing had touched all creation.

And this new man who had come, who had flown in her plane, who had suddenly been seized by the gasp of fright which she could not but catch, but then had called on something, someone – but not the Mission God – to strengthen him, what was he? Perhaps he had spoken truth. I could not tell, Naburdja thought in a part of the dance when she was back as herself. He is not of us. He is not of the other Australians. It seems he is doing what he said he would do – looking for and finding plants, treating them gently, writing their names. But do we believe in this? With a stranger it is not safe to take the word from the mouth. Better to pick up the true thoughts when you can. Although he was afraid in the plane there was no wish to hurt. And his strengthener is who – what? A rainbow? A flood coming through the rock gates? Some kind of mother? No, not entirely any of these. Perhaps that answer will come, Naburdja said to herself while her feet and her body went on dancing.

At dawn she moved slowly across, touching other dancers on the way, her ankle feathers brushing against theirs; light grew in the sky; the stars dwindled, were no longer there, but the hollow was still dark and the grandmothers were almost as asleep as the small children. Naburdja lay down briefly alongside her own child, her eyelids flickered shut, the two skins melted together in love and rest. She smelled her girl child totally, as the child, sleeping, became enclosed in her mother's smell. In the night nobody could have parted one black skin from the other, but as

99

the dawn light began to filter down, the palm of the child's hand, limp and upturned, would have seemed a little lighter, her hair with a reddish tinge. It was always so; the total black skin glow, the startling black wave of hair, only came to the adult. The child was too fragile to bear it.

Naburdja stayed close and resting, breathing deep in the rhythm of complete relaxation in which she ceased to be merely human and became instead all the beings she had danced herself into. When she felt the early sun on her shoulder she drew herself away; the child still slept. One day the child too would dance; now she was dreaming it, caught from her mother.

Naburdja slipped into her jeans and began to run, her long legs taking another new, easy rhythm. Her body was filled with power and comfort. One day, she said to herself, I will pilot a space ship. She thought of this space ship in English technical words. She had seen detailed videos, talked to pilots. Piloting in space is different, I know that, I shall have to learn, but yes, I will do that. But I shall also, always, come back. She began to analyze the thoughts that had come to her about the newcomer who had told them he had only come for plants. Best to speak with Djiuvalji. She turned her thoughts hard onto him.

They met in the usual place; a crack in the hills had opened long ago in the dreamtime. In the wet a stream from behind, from far off, grew, pushed, struggled against stones, foamed over and burst through. For hours or sometimes days it foamed and spread out, making a great noise; then suddenly it was over. But now, even in the dry, there remained a dark pool completely over-shadowed, going deep. On the rocks were drawings. But these were not to be looked at lightly, without preparation. Naburdja sat under a river-gum that grew so shiningly, sucking on the deeply buried water. She and the river-gum itself were small, toy entities below the vast and shocking cliffs. But Djiuvalji

100

saw them from a long way off. They spoke now in their own language, first with formal greetings which set accurately the relationship between them, then down to the main point. 'I ask,' she said, 'does that one understand?'

'Not yet. But he eats our food. Gladly. He does not ask for the other kinds. He thinks about our plants.'

'To eat?'

'No, no, to put into a pattern which is in his mind but also in books. That is, a pattern of knowing how the plants fit together. So that some are close sisters and others – have different ancestors. He finds which can marry and which are forbidden.'

'He thinks, then, sideways: plants – people. But with respect? Not to tear them up and plant bread corn?'

'I believe not. When he finds a new plant which he does not know, it is as if he speaks to it and welcomes it. I have watched him. That is good, I think?'

Naburdja tried to picture this man more fully. 'But in his patterns. In his thinking. Perhaps he could be guided?'

'Is it possible – he could be a bridge? I too have thought.'

They looked at one another. Djuvalji scraped his foot along the ground as though feeling deep into it. At last Naburdja said: 'I am not the only pilot. I can take time if it is for something good. Yet – the others who have become bridge people – they share blood with us. They can slip out from whiteness and the ancestors know them. But he?'

'It seems to me – ' Djiuvalji frowned; it was difficult to find the words. ' – that if the one who is a bridge can – can make the jump himself – then all goes well. The ancestors are satisfied. They open the dreaming to him.' Naburdja nodded agreement. He went on: 'He asks and asks, this one. Sometimes I think I have said too much.'

'We must be careful. This is not an outside thing like – like an

101

engine. Can he listen to what is inside? Without hurting it – or himself?'

'I think so. Even the things I have told him, carefully, yes, he folds them up, he puts away gently. There is also this. He is not one of the Mission people, he does not want to catch us and make us different and have other kinds of hope. It seems that he has some kind of inside thing himself, but he does not let it interfere with others. All peoples have their own magic and their own music. Yet we can speak with one another.'

'Speaking is not enough.'

'No. But it goes far and deep, if the speakers choose.'

'I see. Now: if we guide him I think we should first show him plants freely, all he wants, and then, a word at a time, as one might treat a healing wound – ' Djiuvalji nodded. Naburdja was holding a spray from a spiky, salty branch, moving her fingers on it without letting it prick her. She went on: 'We would have to test him, several times. To see if all goes well. Like you must test an engine. That takes a short time if you are careful. It is longer for a human person. It is longer for – for the test of our way of living. Thousands of years.'

'Yes,' said Djuvalji, 'Many thousands. Back to the dreaming which is the proof. Forward and back. Will he ever see this?'

'Who knows' said Naburdja, 'but for his own sake we must try.'

'And perhaps for ours if – if Darwin was to become – hurtful.'

She looked up frowning, fixed on something far off. 'Yes. They might. Somehow. Though I think – I hope – that in the end they would know us and respect us as Australians. But – yes, I too have felt it, a tease, a hardness, when I grounded there the last two, three times.'

'Be careful then,' said Djuvalji, 'you are very valuable. To all of us. Try to find how they will be at Darwin before you are there next.'

102

He spoke anxiously, but she shook her head. 'I cannot feel them in Darwin. I cannot lock in. But with this new man – a little, already.'

'Good' said Djulvalji in English and then both stayed quiet, their hands on the lifting bark of the great tree, listening to one another's thoughts stretching and rebounding and steadying.

# CHAPTER FIFTEEN

Rahul opened his eyes, for a moment uncertain of where he was. Or who he was. The noise of voices and the crackle of flames had died away and there was a first dream. The taps of the music sticks had gone on, thin and accurate, but no, they were something else, they were the great Natural Orders, the Families, the Genera, the Species. The Taxonomy spread dazzlingly, lines crossing, merging, expanding into infinity. He grasped them in one hand, from far back, from before the forests of the coal measures, through to remotest future. It was his, all plants grew from him. And then the lines tangled, they slid away, they became drops of crystal, touching, blinding, not there. He fell head foremost through a river of crystals into the second dream. He had been there. There.

But the memory raced away along the lines of taxonomy, away, away. He tried to remember, it had been important, there had been largenesses, shapes in the second dream. In it everything had been explained, it was all working out. In the end he would see the pattern, he would understand. He had felt immense encouragement, certainty, trust. Yes, it was still there, wrapping him round, but wherever, whatever, whoever it came from, had vanished, had receded as the tapping of the music sticks had receded into silence, had become a pin point of light somewhere inside himself. But could grow, could flower – if he knew how –

Djiuvalji was speaking to him, apparently questioning him, but the question had not made itself clear. He smiled at Djiuvalji, acknowledging the question, but waiting for the answer to come out of the crystal point. It seemed that Djiuvalji was no longer wearing shirt and trousers, as he had been – when? He was naked, but painted all over in wavy lines, so much better than being clothed, for the paint rippled engagingly as he moved. The patterns were as real as dreams. Yes, Djiuvalji was painted as something, someone, out of the second dream, the deep one. Was it the turtle? And if so, what exactly was it, the turtle *is*? Is it the turtle *was*? He must shake his mind awake into the world of people, of Djiuvalji and himself and the other men. Djiuvalji was wearing the familiar arm bands and also feather bands on his ankles and some kind of thing slung round his neck. Yes, everything was beginning to come clear.

'Where are you?' Djiuvalji asked.

'Here' said Rahul, 'Now, waking. Alive.'

'Where you been?' Djiuvalji asked again, fixing his eyes.

'In dreaming,' Rahul answered. 'Good dreaming. My plants. I understood everything.'

Djiuvalji laughed. 'Who told you? Who you see there?'

'Don't know. Forget.' Rahul said. He looked down at his fingers, surprised at their unleafiness. Not roots: nails.

Yet it seemed that Djiuvalji had been in some way aware. 'You

104

been a plant' he said. 'Growing. That was good, I think. Very good.'

Rahul began to laugh; it was all so funny. A short shower of crystals enveloped him, then dispersed. And he had no headache, nothing nasty. If they could so easily dip themselves into this ocean of understanding, of encouragement, of happiness, what need for alcohol? Or cannabis or opium or soma or any other drug? What need for governments and schools? True, you have to learn the way; he had been guided by Djiuvalji and Naburdja. 'But where is Naburdja?' he asked.

'Other side,' said Djiuvalji quickly. 'You don't ask.'

'Oh sorry, sorry!' said Rahul and again found himself laughing. He ought to have remembered that the women's camp was over the ridge, behind the enormous rock with the paintings which he did not yet fully understand, out of sight. There would equally be delightful and interesting things being worked out by those others. Naburdja would be in her own dream which she would understand. In both camps strict rules were being followed with a view to one known end: he himself was most fortunate to have been led by the hand.

He began to remember. Yes, he had taken off his shirt and trousers as they had told him to do. He had unwound his turban and his dark uncut Sikh hair had flowed round his shoulders and down his back. Perhaps he had felt the paint being put upon him. But by now he was looking very intensely at a rock picture, the symbols of the going through in which every dot counted. As in real life but enlarged, deified, though not in the clumsy Caucasian way or the over-sophisticated Dravidian way. But other and intensifying at every breath. Yes, it was a different kind of intensity from the one he might have used, cutting himself off from outside interruptions in a botanical investigation. Or just thinking: thinking scientifically. Thinking, as it is sometimes but not always, practised by educated people. And then the self, behind all that intensifying, disappeared. Yes, yes, he thought flashingly, and so it worked and he had gone through. Through and on.

Now he stood up: no dizziness, no nausea, instead an improved overall feeling, a heightening of perception. How clear the light! How sharp the line of rock ridges, bare, orange, untouched except by the secret painters! Beyond the great yellow plain lay hot and still, dotted with bushes, grey-green, hard, spiky. The black arms and legs of his friends were like drawings in Indian ink, like the black swans on the blue lakelets of Victoria, far away to the south. Yet some were a light golden-brown, not even as dark as he himself was, with golden glints in their hair, very heterozygous. One of Naburdja's friends was almost a white Australian, but yet she had the blood of three generations back and had called herself in. There they all were, having this experience, as he too had been allowed it out of their great courtesy. He glanced at the small cut on his own arm: nothing. He was still wearing his bracelet on the wrist; they had agreed, it was his private magic. He had tried to explain that all Sikhs wore such bracelets – but that hadn't registered. Never mind.

He looped back his un-cut hair and went over to the big fire. There was a great fish wrapped in leaves and roasted, bony but tasty, and several roots, eatable but not particularly good. The big fish spears, each differently decorated, were sloped against a tree trunk: what a game fish spearing was! There were several kinds of eggs and unbeatable wild honey. Freefood would probably have been sweet potatoes or some of the yams, even ordinary potatoes, all slightly preferable to the wild roots. But the fruit and nuts were delicious and interesting; Freefood wouldn't have bothered to grow them. There would only have been dreary old bananas and oranges and pineapples, the obvious things for the semi-tropics. Not that a mango wouldn't be nice. Perhaps we have them; they would probably go wild here once they got a hold. But every meal he had joined in seemed to be different and because of that, a new experience, usually a pleasure.

At another fire they were gobbling roasted lizards; someone was singing. He went over. At first they had thought – and he thought himself – that this could not possibly be one of his tastes. But it was a taste he'd acquired and he crunched away and everyone was talking and eating and there were plenty more lizards. He recognized the song now; it was a formalized story of a boy's voyage to magic Macassa, long, long ago. Higher up, among the rocks, someone was sounding away on the strange pipe, the didgeridoo; it was like the waves of heat passing over still sand. Like something at the back of one's mind. In the dream.

On the edge of the great camp the emus stopped or ran, their flat, golden-eyed heads with room for one thought only: food. Everywhere, in and out of sight again, there were flights of the flower-coloured parakeets. River-gums grew along the dry sand flood plain of whatever sudden river swept seasonally down; here were pairs of beautiful galahs. Possums bobbed in and out of sight. Plenty of tucker for people without disturbing any of their living visitors.

At still another fire there was maize porridge for those who liked it, from the cultivated fields that a few family groups, mostly quarter-castes from further south, had started. They had of course contributed their food, but not everyone cared for it. He didn't himself, though he took a little on a leaf, for courtesy's sake, adding a dab of tamarind – another non-native, but well-established. They might accept a little help here: a better strain of maize, a few more spices. Cloves perhaps. They had planted coconuts too, but they were not yet bearing. The great thing is, he thought, that people are allowed to do very much what they want to do, so long as they keep to the Rules. He himself could not know the Rules, but he could make a guess at them; they were meant to preserve the patterns of the natural world in this Australian eco-system and its interpretation. Which might be correct.

And he had written to Anne, and the letter would be on its way, perhaps already there, at the Centre. And everything, he knew, would be all right. All this would go on, the control situation, the control population. The Board would certainly realize its importance, its essential relevance, once Anne explained it. Anne Tomlin, F.R.S., the authority. Dear Anne, oh my dear Anne, almost my mother!

# CHAPTER SIXTEEN

In the last year or two there had been some trouble from anti-morphogenesis groups, ranging from those in America who said it was against God's Will and intentions towards His creatures, to those in the fussier parts of northern Europe who complained that things no longer tasted as they should, especially all-the-year-round imported fruit. Yes, they said, it was free, yes, the fruit was bigger, perhaps better coloured, but do you remember the taste of our own strawberries, the Singa Sengane, ah, they melted in the mouth! Or do you remember our berry picking expeditions into the mountains, cloudberries, cranberries, blueberries, part of our lives and our parents' and grandparents', essential to health, to the autumn build-up against the frost giants? Soon enough we'd have our skis out again, but there was the memory of the sun on our backs as we stooped over the berry bushes between the carpets of reindeer moss, the sparkle of the red in our baskets, the scented shimmer of the blue. Why should we take these stupid oranges and bananas, these tasteless apples and raspberries, these foreign mangoes and pineapples that have no memories for us?

However, this was not serious. If the Norwegians affected to despise the Freefood and go off crawling up their mountains with their little berry baskets, it was no concern of the Board, and in any case they could not grow nearly enough food grains or vegetables for their population, so they were as dependent for essentials as the rest. In fact it was only in a very few favoured and under-populated parts of the tropics that there was normally so much indigenous food to be had for the picking or fishing that nobody could be bothered to collect the Freefood from the depots. The excuse usually was that it was difficult to cook, the women didn't like it. But such happy places did not count.

So here and there, a kind of minor unease spread. It seemed that many people's favourite occupations had been almost totally devalued, especially in the very large border areas between the totally urban life and the classic country life, rare enough as this latter had become in the developed world. Many millions of fairly vocal semi-urban people still had gardens and even allotments in some countries so how did it affect them? What was the good now of growing the biggest gooseberry or the longest cucumber? What pleasure even for the perfect or novel rose or sweet pea, the award winner, when the laboratory manipulated plants were inevitably superior to one's own, however much thought and skill one had put into the months and years of plant care? A certain kind of happiness had withered away and would, it seemed, never come back and could never be replaced.

But this was not all. It had become apparent that PAX was involved in more than feeding people. For a time there was talk of monopolies but it died down; what other body could feed this world? Naturally, controls had been necessary in order to grow the food – which quite often meant displacing other kinds of plant life – and move it where it was needed. But one control leads to another. For the sake of convenience and efficiency, as the Board was careful to point out. And also in order to avoid too many uncertainties in the computer instructions. Not for power, no impossible! The Board was totally non-political, for nobody in their senses could say that feeding the hungry was a political act when it was so clear to the whole Board that it was a moral one.

All the same, that was exactly what they did say. There were the groups which had been in food production or distribution themselves and, even if they had been bought out at what had appeared at the time to be a reasonable price, often including shares in PAX, there was now a diminishing field for re-investment and the market games which had been so exciting and profitable. Nor was it only the food industry. For it seemed that most primary production had become part of the same network, as well as much in the way of engineering, transport, basic chemicals, power sources and increasingly the leisure industries in their various shapes. For many people this rationalisation, as the Board explained it, seemed to have something wrong about it. Not human. Too big. And there were no proper channels of complaint, even if they could be put into a sensible, money-conscious statistic-based form. The western-type, liberal governments made it clear that it was none of their business. Some other governments had so much identified with

PAX, especially since that world-resounding Nobel prize, that they let it be known that complaints were not in order.

The Board was not unduly worried. Nothing had been done which could be considered against the highest canons of financial propriety. In earlier days Sir Edmund had met and, in fact, got the better of several rivals or opponents of whose business ethics he disapproved. Great companies often turned out to have shady under-sides. In the long run these usually endangered the parent body, made it vulnerable. But now he, and PAX, were out of all that. They were quite content simply to grow. That, at least, was how he felt when meeting the Board.

Harnam and his friends at Ideas had been working on the story of a dissident group, sympathetically represented, special subliminals and so on – and how in the end, by deep understanding and almost agreement, they were won over – and happy. Happy with everyone else – with all the world, it had been a most moving experience for all the producers and advisers. They had talked it over afterwards, getting a real high. Something that would show the Board what they could do, how well spent the salaries of Ideas were! Harnam was so delighted with the first private showing – dear old Marie-Claire had been there too – that he simply had to hop the first plane over and tell his mother. Ah, Nandu! As always he felt what a waste that he had not been able to be her role-instructor in some super production, even now – but what she must have been like thirty years ago!

But his mother seemed uneasy. After a little questioning it came out that there had been a letter from Rahul to his father. Saranjit had, apparently, been very much disturbed. 'But perhaps that has been good for him,' said Nandu, 'at least he is exercising his mind instead of staying in the dumps.'

'What did the letter say?' asked Harnam.

'Well,' she said, 'I was not properly told and I did not read it

111

and he has gone off to the office block with the letter scrunched up in his palm, you know, but I think, yes I am sure, it was about certain people who have refused the food.'

'Some do,' said Harnam, 'but it does not matter at all if they waste their money buying something else. After all, most things that people want have come – partly at least – from ourselves. From PAX. So in the end they give us their money!'

'But these were poor people' she said.

'Oh,' said Harnam, 'then they have been led astray. Perhaps by stupid priests. Or by agitators. Rahul was, I think, in Australia. The Board has had rude messages from that Professor Ritchie. Perhaps he met Rahul.'

'Yes' said Nandu, 'they met. But Rahul did not like him. He too said there was a rudeness. Rahul should come home. It is time. He should marry. As you also should do. Your sisters are so happy.'

But Harnam dodged this. He said 'It is not good when even small groups of people break away from us, especially the poor. That looks bad. It shows there is a flaw. Perhaps a mis-understanding.' He shook his head. 'And we are doing such a great thing! Why can they not see it?'

Yes, thought Nandu, my son should be married and have something better to do and then he will think less about this Freefood. Which I do not like. And it is getting more difficult to buy the special things which I need in my kitchen and which are not included in this nonsense that the men have invented, not understanding that a small amount of this or that is necessary for good cooking, though not perhaps for rough health. When they come to my table, naturally any sensible woman knows at once that I use such things, as she probably does herself, though not that stupid Zeenat with her ideas about chemicals inside food. But my dear, wise, noble, unpractical Saranjit does not know because he is above such matters and he even tells people what good meals can be made out of these uninteresting things he has invented! And her elder son believing in it all too! Or so he says. 'If you were to take your parents' advice and marry a nice girl, above all if you would allow us to help just a small bit in this matter, instead of looking cross which does not suit you, I am sure it would help your dear father's depression.'

'That still goes on?' said Harnam, getting her onto another line.

'Yes' she said, 'it does.' She shook her head sadly.

'Do you think – if he were to see a Swami?' Harnam asked. 'We have one at Ideas. Very modern. Very tuned in.'

'No, no, that would only upset your poor father. He will not even see a doctor. He says to me his work is no more good.'

'That is – oh, that is genuine stuff-and-nonsense. He might as well say that Freefood is no good.'

'He does say that' said Nandu, 'and perhaps he may be correct!'

# CHAPTER SEVENTEEN

'Oh fuck!' said Neil Ritchie unoriginally and read through the note on his desk. 'Fuck; bugger; fuck. Can't these fucking bastards ever leave me alone! I've got *work!*'

Fred, used to this, strolled over. 'No need to do a thing, Boss. Just reckoned you ought to know, to give it a look-see. I'll handle it.' He felt, even, that it would make a nice change from dealing with those sets of figures the comp. kept spewing out. And the girl who brought them in no great shakes. Not like Judith-Ann used to be. And how's she getting on with that new bloke of hers?

Neil Ritchie was calming down. He only hit his desk once. 'Look,' he said, 'these fucking morons of bureaucrats up in Darwin, which is lousier with them than Canberra even, believe you me, they've got a pile of Freefood that the Abos refuse to take and why the fuck shouldn't they!'

'Right-oh, the Abos probably eat well when there's food and die off when there isn't. Sensible, keeps the gene strain on its toes. I don't see what it's got to do with us.'

'Nor it has. Nor it bloody has! But everyone keeps on pushing me around. The Board – '

'They haven't got far with pushing you, Boss.'

'I should hope not. I told them where to get off!' He was beginning to shoot out great puffs of laughter. 'Interesting about those Abos refusing the food. I remember that bloke of Judith-Ann's talking about it. The way they thought about their food. You know, Billy-boy's been around, wanting to speak to me.'

'Has he now! Did he bring the kid?'

'I saw the kid, yes. Seemed fine. Confident. Easy. Amusing himself. Talking to anyone. Nice kid. Bloke wanted me to tell Judith-Ann. Which I haven't done. Not till she's settled with her new bloke who wasn't that keen on the kid.'

Fred was a bit shocked. 'Look, Boss, Billy-boy stole that kid. You ought to have called in the police, nabbed him!'

'Ought I? Well now, Fred, that's funny, that kind of thought never crossed my mind.' He shook his head owlishly. 'I'm a bad old man.' Fred scuffed with his shoe, abashed and bothered. What was the Boss up to? Cunning old bugger. 'You can answer

114

Darwin,' said Neil Ritchie. 'Give them something that'll keep them quiet.' He smiled. Fred went out and composed a reply.

Then other things came up. Fred had some ideas ticking away at the back of his mind; he'd like to show them to the Boss, but not quite yet. There was not much doing at the moment, mostly routine, answering queries from the Sinai group, telewatching the work in the Sahara and briefly remembering the old man's remark about the rehabilitation of deserts looking good but apt to change the weather, not always to total benefit for other populations. When he came back, with soothing remarks ready and hoping to have a little chat about his own ideas, he found a note to himself from the Boss: 'Gone walkabout. Bak Son' and signed 'Eeyore'. 'Bak Son' indeed! Silly old bastard, getting it wrong, ought to have been Pooh. Or was it Wol? Yes, Wol it was! Years since he'd read that stupid Pommy book, but it stuck in his mind. But maybe old Neil did it on purpose. Identifying with Eeyore. Who gets put upon, but always survives. Was it that? You never knew. Not with Neil Ritchie. Nor what 'soon' meant: tomorrow? A year's time? You never knew. Why do we go on working for him, some of us? Don't know that, either.

No, you never knew, not with Neil Ritchie. Nor how his temper would be when you came across him next.

At his next reappearance it was Rahul who was agreeably surprised, especially after last time. He had been sent for to the gate. It was not clear to him how the message had come, certainly not by the little plane which, quite soon, came to pick him up. Nor yet by anything in the nature of radio, telephone or what-not. He was far from all the methods of that kind. However by now he was used to means of communication which did not conform to normal scientific or industrial standards. But someone he did not know at all but whom he suspected of being a turtle, had walked up and told him he was needed at the gate 'for Ritchie'. In turn

115

he had asked Naburdja, before take-off, what it was about and how she had heard, but she smiled and said 'Open way, telephone, to me. You, our friend, you heard on shut way.'

'But how – ' he began, only then she motioned him into the plane and took her own seat. He was pleased that now he had no hesitation at all about flying with her as pilot; he settled into complete and pleasant trust, and a cool and comfortable seat. He had not quite adapted to sitting for a long time on his haunches as his new friends did, not even cross-legged which would have suited Indian joints rather better. There was one stop before the gate, at a settlement, scattered, mostly decorated shelters with small children running in and out naked or slightly painted, but a few solid mud-brick buildings and a well kept air strip. Why shouldn't cultures mix? So long as one doesn't destroy another.

It was the beginning of the wet and ahead of them the floods were creeping brown and greenish along all hollows. Three or four passengers had joined at the settlement, one an almost white woman, rather beautiful, with a darker baby. They were looking out on both sides; the woman was nervous, pulling her seatbelt tight and clutching at the baby till it cried. The plane rose quickly, circling up to reach a layer above the dark thunder clouds; it was unpressurized but the clouds were low, pressing onto the land, ready to burst. As they tilted up Rahul noticed that he was meshing in to Naburdja as she did quick calculations, glancing at her clock faces and making little adjustments. Part of it was reassurance for her younger co-pilot who had joined at the settlement. Part was mathematics, though not expressed in the kind of forms Rahul had been used to, either at school or talking about spirals with Anne in the old days. Naburdja seemed to have some kind of rapport with – what? As they dived through openings with dark and enormous clouds towering round them, moving to enclose or thinning out, she seemed to know within

116

herself, confidently, what was happening, and to be able to choose the right path.

Once and then again, the plane shook and jarred as lightning was momentarily all about them, but they were through, as a little fly escapes from a hand clap. Survival was the thing, survival through delicate understanding of natural forces, over hundreds of thousands of generations in an environment where those same natural forces were what had to be watched and known. So why not use this new understanding on the new cloud way? Now she dived the plane down through a valley, a narrow cleft between ballooning, changing cloud cliffs, rain-grey, and at the end clear sky again. He caught her thanks in her mind output and joined in as far as he could. Then, as they circled down and down, he caught a glimpse of the straight road in from Darwin and the outside world, and probably Neil Ritchie. Enough to make anyone feel nervous!

'Well, well,' said Neil Ritchie, his hands in his pockets, grinning a bit, 'so you're the one to say if I'm a villain or not. Now I wonder, would you know?'

'This is – unexpected,' said Rahul, and then 'Perhaps you would be good enough to tell me why you are here.'

'Interest, sheer bloody interest. Billy-boy and the kid and I, we came along. Funny thing, Rahul, I got bored looking at all that wheat.'

One of the men at the gate was talking quietly to 'Billy-boy' in a language Rahul didn't know. The kid was being passed round, kissed and cuddled and loved. He would hardly get as much from a mother with a job or a new husband. Naburdja – but now Rahul knew it was only an outside name – leaned against the plane, her white pilot's overalls shiningly clean, as were her teeth as she smiled. He took in the bright shine of health, of cleanness and confidence on her dark face which had once seemed definitely unpleasing, but was now pleasant and familiar. As was her mind.

For a few minutes Neil Ritchie and Rahul held a kind of conversation, not yet arriving anywhere definite, rather getting to know one another in a new and different situation. There was news to be passed on, also some discussion of botany. Suddenly Rahul said: 'Look, Neil, have you come here as a friend? You know perfectly well what I mean. Isn't that so?'

'Yes,' said the Boss, 'I think I could agree to that. People who refuse to be pushed around – bound to be all right, yes! By the way, Rahul, what's that name I hear them calling you?'

Rahul didn't answer at once, then said slowly: 'That, yes. That's my country name. Viridja. It's the name for people who can make outside things into something acceptable to Murngin. I wonder what yours would be. Supposing –'

'Ah' said Neil, 'so it's like that. O.K. I'm coming in.'

'If they let you.'

'Oh, they'll let me all right.' He looked round. Naburdja nodded, and so did the men at the gate. Neil Ritchie's walkabout had got him where he had intended. Perhaps now he was unlikely to go back soon.

# CHAPTER EIGHTEEN

A small group from the anti-morphogensis movement arrived at the Centre. Their plane had landed on the beautiful green strip between the damp, breathing trees – it was that time of year; everything smelled of growth. They shed their coats and waited while Anne was told of their arrival. She had been impatient at first, not wanting to be interrupted. Then looking again and with some surprize at the names on the delegation, she said yes, yes, of course. One was an old colleague, others were names she knew and respected; one or two had been at Royal Society soirees in the days when she used to go to them – a good while ago. She told one of the staff to see that the plane was well stocked up with fruit, nuts and sambals for the return journey.

At the same time she tried to get Saranjit to come over, but he was unavailable. Nandu had mixed in some bhang – not a Freefood distribution! – in his favourite curry, hoping it would have some happy effect. It had certainly lightened his depression, and he supposed himself to have made some important discoveries. He was far too deeply occupied with computering these to take any notice of Anne's message. Somehow the computer, not having had a dose of bhang fed into it, was refusing to give the answer that Saranjit demanded of it. However he was now being very affectionate to his wife, which was a good sign or so she thought.

Meanwhile the delegation had settled themselves on the chairs and settees all round Anne's own office; it was low Indian-fashion furniture, mostly her grandfather's, with covers of hand-woven Orissa cotton, each of them with a different design of stylized flowers and animals, still whole and handsome after half a century of wear and washing. There were some fine rugs too and the ceiling fans were going strongly. When Anne came in the discussion started, all very reasonably and properly. Soon she found herself more in agreement with them than she would have liked. Nobody denied the good effects on world health and probably on peace-keeping, due to the Freefood and perhaps some other activities of PAX. What worried them, as it did her, was the curious sense of loss which was affecting so many areas of life, including scientific research. Yes, certainly there were great problems yet to be unravelled. Doubtless she knew about many of them. There had been glances at the books and journals which were lying round and an open pencil-marked copy of *Nature*. But even with these problems the interest was becoming more spasmodic, especially among the younger people who had lived entirely in the Freefood world. It was a curious damping down effect. Not so bad for those who had taken to space in some of its aspects. But the biological sciences – 'even history seems to have slowed down' said another, half laughing.

'So, my dear Dr Tomlin,' said one of her old acquaintances, 'it seems to appear as a question of what more is worthwhile doing or being when so much is almost effortlessly supplied? What has happened to individual hopes and struggles of all kinds?'

'Look,' said Anne, 'is this altogether the fault of Freefood?'

'Not directly,' said the leading speaker of the group, 'it is rather the taking away of individual responsibility for something basic. Going back to the beginning of man as a social animal. Handing it over to – others.'

'Us' said Anne, but meaning Them, as some of the Delegation guessed.

'At the back of all our history: food' another member said. She was an old school fellow of Anne's, now a highly respected sociologist. She added: 'I think you probably know all our arguments and equally probably you are in at least partial agreement with them. But your own research is so involved that you find it difficult to take a dispassionate view. Am I right?'

'In a way' said Anne, uncomfortably, because she was beginning to feel guilty, knew that was stupid and unreal, but all the same . . .

120

The talk went on. The possibility of something going wrong on a large scale came up, and this reminded Anne that there had been a video about some mysterious illness – could it even have been death? – somewhere in the Pacific. But that might have been a rumour or some kind of religious aberration. She hadn't paid much attention because she had been working at a rather fascinating set of figures. And then someone raised the possibility of people genuinely refusing the Freefood, not just supplementing it with food they preferred or grew themselves, perhaps for sentimental reasons – they were candidly admitting that possibility – but totally refusing to allow it to be brought in. A whole town, for instance, doing that. Or a rural district. Doing it in order to see if – well, in fact, if they would be happier.

'But happiness isn't easy to measure' said Anne. 'There are no markings.' Yet all the same she admitted the possibility. It was an argument she had heard before. Happiness? For a moment she drifted back to a rather delightful and unexpected pick-up, a Malaysian girl who had come over to learn a particular technique which the laboratory at the Centre had optimized. She had begun by admiring Anne, and then had caught a secret look. And then – When I put those deepest pink and purple orchids into her hair, Anne remembered, that slight colour change where they reflected on her cheek bones. So soft. Orchids her native flower, she had said, lisping a little. Faithless? Of all meaningless words! Yes, a strictly temporary but quite acute happiness. Not measurable. And of course not encroaching on Marie and that other deep down happiness. Why should it?

She switched to the group, who were trying out definitions. Certainly they had something. They were putting into words and organized statements the doubts which had been gnawing at her for so long. But always half suppressed. The thesis that things were getting to be, in a certain sense, too easy. Food, the essen-

121

tial need round which all societies have been based, through all the human and for that matter the proto-human millenia, when we were developing our food-catching hands, our ears to listen for deer or grubs, our forward looking eyes and our getting together for hunting and gathering and at last harvesting. Take away that basic need or rather transmute it into a solid security about which there was no point in planning or organizing, and what happens to the patterns of society, the loyalties and responsibilities, the hopes and fears? And suddenly it all tied in with Rahul's letter. Yes, it tied in so neatly that it was like a piece of mathematics.

All at once it boiled over in her mind. 'I see what you are after,' she said, 'and curiously enough it is part of our overall world plan. We intend to have something in the nature of a control group which is not to have the Freefood distributed to it. We intend to watch how such a group – such a society – develops and how it compares with the normal groups who get the Freefood. But I am telling you this in confidence – ' She looked round the delegation ' – and I must ask you to keep it entirely to yourselves. It has not yet been made public.'

They nodded solemnly, voicing agreement not to speak of this most interesting development. They were responsible people, not young tearaways and it was flattering to be trusted. But naturally Anne Tomlin would recognize this, in fact had done so handsomely. Only one had, to Anne's knowledge, any close contacts with the media. A very strong look passed. The lady murmured that there would be no leak, and was rewarded with a special smile.

'This is really very good news,' said the leader of the delegation, a distinguished anthropologist. 'May I ask, where is this control group likely to be located?'

122

'I don't think Sir Edmund has quite made up his mind,' said Anne sweetly.

'So it was the Chairman of your Board himself! Yes, yes. A very remarkable man. Very.'

'Perhaps I might say: not in Europe' said Anne.

'Well, well. That is probably sensible policy.'

'Yes. We would expect that: your Chairman springs the most astonishing surprises' said another.

'I can quite imagine that working with him is most rewarding.' Yet another!

'I don't think we can have any more profitable discussion, do you?' said Anne. She thought she might laugh if it went on. She added: 'Perhaps I have told you more than I should have.'

'Not at all, not at all! We do realize now that the problems and anxieties which have been so much in our minds are also in yours. And indeed, in those of the PAX Board. Something of a comfort. A control community – somewhere . . . ' The delegation said friendly goodbyes and went back to their plane which had meantime taken on baskets of mangoes, several kinds of banana and as many pawpaws as they could possibly manage, as well as enormous bunches of lilies.

Anne waved. So this is what's going to happen, she said, half aloud, how very odd. But if Saranjit had been there I couldn't have done it. He doesn't enjoy lying. A non-Sikh thing probably! She considered herself; yes, she rather enjoyed the occasional small lie so long as it was not about work. But this one, well, this one was going to be fact. She nodded at the open copy of *Nature*.

# CHAPTER NINETEEN

It was never plain sailing for long with the Board. Perhaps it would have been dull if it had been, instead of being so gripping that the man who had once been insignificant Ed Green without a care in the world (but was he remembering inaccurately?) could no longer get free of Board matters and didn't even want to. As a man gets older he stops being distracted by those emotional disturbances which at the time seemed so desirable. His power of concentration grows correspondingly. He knows the moment to switch. He can slow down events or hurry them. He can contradict himself if necessary without this becoming apparent. He is in a totally creative condition. God-like? Well, he would hardly say that. Only that here was his real pleasure.

The pleasure of problems was dealing with them. It looked now as if there had been trouble in parts of the Pacific. Ethel Gabani had sent a disturbing cable about unexplained deaths on her own island which had been receiving large shipments of the newly improved taro, as well as the new yams which they had taken to in a big way. They had tried to reach her on video, but it was out of order at her end, not for the first time. Probably it had nothing to do with the Freefood but it would have to be cleared up. Dr Ikewa, the Japanese Board member, was particularly interested: there was a food overlap with some of the further-out Japanese islands. Ikewa was one of the new members. It was not unwelcome to have a fresh mind on the Board with a new set of opinions. Not that all new board members had that, especially the political appointments. The Chairman could think of several but fortunately they did not always attend.

He looked round. Ferguson never had any new ideas now and his hair had receded noticeably. However, he could be trusted to follow up a point well after it had been made.

Gustavsen was putting on weight: bad for the mind, that. Probably Dr Schulmann had aged as little as any; she had never looked any particular age. And the Raffray, ah yes, the Raffray, she was still mentally flexible. But was she totally loyal, totally his? She had been the most upset over what had reached them about the Pacific deaths. That came of having too much imagination. None of us had better allow ourselves to imagine what is happening in the Gabani's island until the facts are before us.

But now, on top of that, had come this curious and really disturbing video from Anne Tomlin. The Chairman had taken it himself since it seemed to have a particular importance. She had begun by reading aloud in a properly professional manner from a letter which, she assured them, *Nature* had agreed to print. That new editor! It was all about the importance of control groups in the Freefood programme. Not implausible as an idea and perhaps worth discussion, though an awkward situation might easily arise if a control group found itself, or pretended to find itself, definitely under-privileged in an oncoming situation. Scarcely democratic. Enough problems without this one. She had also spoken about the socio-moral problems which Freefood was bringing, not that this would be in the letter. But social morality is always changing! And ought to change, he thought angrily.

This however, was not all. Apparently Anne Tomlin was proposing control groups in terms of whole populations and finished by suggesting – or was it demanding? – as a starting point the aboriginal inhabitants of Arnhem Land or as it now was, Murngin – these names! – exactly where, as he understood from the agents at Darwin, the trouble lay. Those natives had been refusing to allow the Freefood in. Had she been got at? These do-gooders, sticking their noses in! Or, almost as possibly, had she in some way got at the aboriginals? She mentioned that

125

her colleague, Dr Saranjit Singh, was in agreement. His own information on that was that Saranjit was in poor health and doing little scientific work. The letter also inferred that it was Board policy. Well! So what was at the back of it? After reading out the letter she had elaborated on it in a somewhat emotional and unscientific manner he thought, talking about the way of life of these aboriginals. Way of life indeed! How did she know? And this suggestion that it would be Board policy – these scientists trying to pull a fast one. On him! On the Board. No, this had to be stopped. He ran the last couple of minutes again. Well, there was the whole thing scrupulously recorded down to the last brush of her palm over a flushed face. No use being angry – though he was. The letter must of course be officially answered. Or in some way – dealt with. He would have to think. And as he thought about it lengthily the final answer to the whole thing had to be a firm no.

The close group of colleagues to whom he showed it had agreed; it was a dangerous precedent. Small control groups, in Scandinavia, say, where people on the whole behaved sensibly, yes, that might be possible. But definitely not whole populations. The Antis would home in on it. You might say that this was an unimportant and reasonably obscure group of people, but the rest of Australia would be understandably furious. As usual he had got nothing useful in the way of a response from Ritchie's group – apparently the old man was away, but other Australian scientists involved, even quite remotely, in nutritional statistics or physiology, or in race relations, were horrified. No doubt, the suggestion went, that a few of the Aboriginal leaders would welcome this idea because, said some of the anthropologists, it would enhance their power and the respect they were given as controllers of rain, fertility and so on. But in the end it would definitely be a retrogressive step, both health wise and in terms of

126

education and progress. The people at Darwin who were, after all, the most closely involved, were definite about this; Queensland was shocked that aboriginal opinion, if you could call it that, had even been consulted. The only opinions which were guardedly in favour came from the Department of Aboriginal Research at Monash which was largely staffed by the people themselves.

As for Anne Tomlin's letter: 'It would be a pity,' said Prof Ferguson, 'if the letter were to be published.'

'Yes,' said Sir Edmund, 'it might be possible to point out to the editor . . . ' He left the sentence unfinished. 'Or perhaps we might persuade the writer that this was not quite the moment.' She is after all, a thoroughly well balanced and responsible person – normally. She could scarcely avoid realizing once it was pointed out, how this idea of hers was calculated to shake the whole base of the organization of which, after all, her centre was an integral part. He looked round. 'If one of us had a word with her, saw what could be done.' He glanced almost imperceptibly at Madame Raffray.

She had not much wanted to take this on, but when it was put to her by Sir Edmund and she realized that a refusal might be really damaging to Anne, she agreed. And once she was in the plane with the familiar pleasure of the green and brown distances rolling up and lessening between her and Anne, she felt she had been right to say yes. Yet from the first moment, or perhaps the moment after when they had loosed their arms from one another's necks and taken the first deep look in the eyes, Anne was wary. 'I know why you've come, Marie' she said, 'and you shouldn't.'

'I come because I love you, cherie, and I don't want you to make mistakes. We could have talked this over and then, I think, you wouldn't have written this letter, or at least not just the way it is. It will be taken up by – well, some very unscientific groups. They'll use it for their own ends.'

'I'm the judge of that, you know,' said Anne and she was deadly serious.

Marie Claire had brought presents, the very special chocolates, a piece of beautiful Finnish glass. Anne caressed it, had a chocolate popped into her mouth, laughed. So long as they were playing together all went well but they could not keep up its fragile balance. 'Surely you can see, my darling, you who can see so far – ' said Marie, bending and unbending Anne's fingers, gently, gently.

But Anne was not listening. 'I've gone on with this for just too long' she said and drew her hand back.

'With me, my darling?' Marie's heart, guts, gave a horrid jump.

Anne leant back, looked at her, teasing, wanting to hurt – a little anyhow: 'Well, whose side are you on?'

'Must you think of it that way – surely not! Not with me!'

But Anne said quietly: 'I have to,' and groped for her spectacles and put them back on.

But they blurred and Marie could not bear to see the tears and answered sharply: 'How can you say that, my own Anne, after – after all we have been ...' and then she too was near tears. 'This isn't a matter of taking sides. It's a matter of thinking what your proposal might mean to other aspects of Board policy with which, I think, you have no disagreement. What it might mean to the Centre itself. You shared our vision of feeding the world, knowing there would be difficulties and disagreements, but they could be overcome. For the sake of something bigger. Wasn't it this way, Anne my darling?'

'Don't let's talk about it, don't let's think about it,' said Anne. 'All I'm sure of is that I won't have the Board using you to get at me!' And Marie Claire had given in – oh, totally. It was better to have arms round one another, a little laughing and petting with the tears assuaged and the anxieties that had caused them, because after all they were together, here and here only, being what they knew to be their true selves.

Then, cruelly, came the interruption, the sharp summons, the quick apology, the event. It was from the Pacific station. Urgent, urgent. The video flashed and crackled. Then it was Ethel Gabani herself, straight at Anne, crying out that her people were dying, the dead children were lying in heaps beside the schools, all her island was going to die – the Freefood, they all ate the Freefood and it is poison, poison! She almost screamed at Anne, then burst into weeping while Anne questioned back the Chief Medical Officer, his dark face twitching with misery as he stood by Ethel, his arm round her. It was the roots, he said, the improved yams, the taro as well, perhaps all the aroids and diascorias. It had been terrible, terrible, a nerve poison, nothing they could do. As she listened Anne felt the first blows of blame coming down on her from within herself, so much worse than from outside.

Marie kept very quiet, horrified. Anne switched to another station. There was more news and worse from other parts of the Pacific. At first it had not been recognized that it was the Food and then it was too late. There had certainly been thousands of deaths. Some of the small islands had not yet got round to modern communications, so their situation was probably worse than the reports. The French islands? Samoa – they didn't know yet. Papua: not much in Port Moresby, the deaths would be in the taro and yam eating villages. Hundreds? Probably thousands again.

Anne turned to Marie: 'Sorry, love, but I must get on to Saranjit. No, you can't help. No, this is serious. Oh, we were wrong to let ourselves be pushed into trying the roots! Thank God we never got on to turnips!'

'But cherie, it was not your fault. You did all the tests – ' But Anne was not listening. She was calling up Saranjit. The beautiful moment had dropped, fallen and dead like a flower in hot sun.

'You must go now, Marie,' Anne had said, 'you can come back later. Yes, we will be in touch. No, *Nature* is publishing my letter. I thought about it carefully and this is definite. And you can tell your chairman not to try and interfere.'

She tiptoed out – that editor must have said something. Edmund would not like it. A pity. Oh, dear Anne! And as she left Saranjit came on the video screen. 'Anne,' he said, 'if this is so we must find out at once what has happened about the potatoes.'

# CHAPTER TWENTY

Bad news kept coming in from various parts of the Southern Pacific area. What had really happened? How and why? At the Centre nobody could settle anything. The media kept on at them trying to get hold of something definite. All very well Anne and Saranjit going dumb: no comment indeed when all the world was commenting! But what had happened, as a matter of sheer nasty fact? Rumours were going round. A small group was developing a Cut Loose from the Board movement. Some went as far as saying Board Out – though it wasn't really rich as a slogan. One of the young botanists had finished painting a satisfactory poster. Another had contacted the geneticists. The essential thing was to find out exactly about their financial dependence on the Board.

They had tried to get Anne to tell them clearly. But it seemed she wasn't too clear herself. The money had always been there, sufficient for anything that had to be done. It was something that had never interested her much. She became flustered. It became clear to the group that the poor old Biddy, however good she still might be at lab work, was not on the ball over finance. They went on to Saranjit and he just kept on talking and talking, as much use as listening to the birds. Perhaps they ought to go straight to one of the anti-morphogenesis groups, whose criticisms had usually been so irritating – most of them didn't know what they were talking about. But surely it hadn't come to that?

Not quite yet. Man or woman, one has to consider one's position. One's salary. And, for some at least, the ongoing piece of research, which might take some time. Plants don't like to be hurried. Nor any life rhythm, however much it offers itself to be understood. But if things got worse, and it looked as if this was just what was happening, well then? If the media tried to pin the blame where it certainly didn't belong? Well, then – No!

But it had all been shaking Anne. She had been sleeping badly, full of doubts that seemed to develop into physical pain. She walked up and down. She looked at charts and figures. They refused to come alive. There had been yet another visit from Marie, this time with Prof Ferguson and Dr Schulman. It had been strictly business-like; she and Marie had only smiled at one another after a brief hand-clasp. The Centre had been totally cleared. And yet, and yet it might somehow have been her own fault. Not in some detail but could it be that there was something basically wrong with the whole Freefood program which she should have seen and stopped. Should she have refused to tackle any of the roots for Freefood, in spite of what the Board wanted?

Should she have even listened to what the Board wanted? But

they always put it so well, so convincingly – and politely. But that was the Chairman. Should we here have kept off any plants with possible toxic qualities, in case somehow there was a slip? But how were we to find plants which could not, for certain, catch us out? As though they wanted to! Those wretched alkaloids in South America, apparently from a legume which normally has the merest trace of toxicity. And now this big blow-up and so many deaths, more and more every hour; whole islands destroyed, whole cultures, these friendly people! And the next time?

Did the Board feel guilty too? But wasn't it all part of a great big guilt? This new disaster, that wasn't all, oh no! Before this, what about the loss of human happiness, what about the opportunities, the creativeness gone? People were fed, yes, no more hunger, but that wasn't good enough. And now – now – yes, she said to herself, there's such a thing as righteous anger. She wiped her eyes, blew her nose, found her spectacles and her pencil and went through to the main room where Saranjit was looking through a bunch of papers which Harnam had sent over to him. 'Saranjit,' she said, 'What are we going to do? Freefood is beginning to kill people. Like famines used to. We can't just sit back.'

'And look at this nonsense!' he said, almost throwing the papers at her, 'viruses from outer space! What they think they can get people to believe! I only hope it was not my Harnam who thought of that one. These Ideas fellows, they have no – no knowledge, no conscience, only wanting, you know, to be cleverer than one another!'

'Covering for the Board,' she said. 'So far they haven't blamed us. But they might. If they got really frightened about their money. Oh, we should never have let them get at us over these damned root crops! Shall we make a list of plants which we consider should be withdrawn?'

He didn't answer for a moment, then said 'Anne, my dear Anne, do you remember right at the beginning how we thought, both of us – am I right – that our work could only be for good?'

'Yes,' she said, and then 'Some of it was. Most of it perhaps. We mustn't forget that. And most of the work which has been done since, not only by us but in our laboratories, that work is – not morally disturbing. Valuable in itself.'

He nodded. 'We must all get in touch, all who are involved, I think. What are the geneticists up to? They won't want to stop.'

'Mayn't be necessary. But we must sort out the cloning.'

'Yes, I'll go over.'

'Feeling better, Saranjit?'

'Me, oh yes, yes, yes. If there is something to do. Perhaps we shall fight the Board. What do you think? Would you fight the Raffray, Anne?'

'She might be on our side. Possibly. By the way, Saranjit, I think you had a letter from Rahul?'

'Yes,' he said, 'with this notion of a control group somewhere in Australia among the savages. I thought it was nonsense. If there were to be control groups they should be in all climates. And we would have recommended them earlier.'

'You thought that. So did I. But now I am convinced that this is the right course. It will have to be done somewhere. Preferably in northern Australia where it would apparently be welcomed. In this way no breaches of agreement need be feared. If this is not successful nutritionally and above all socially, it need not be repeated. However, if it is, control groups might be started at a later stage in other climatic and social conditions. You see?' She waited for Saranjit to take this in. He gulped slightly; it had happened once or twice in the past that Anne, usually so careful to keep him informed, as he had been – he hoped – with her, had suddenly done something on her own. She went on: 'In fact I have written to *Nature*. Yes, it has been accepted.'

'Without consulting me, Anne!' He was a little plaintive.

'You were not interested. Remember? When I mentioned my letter from Rahul you brushed it aside because, as you said just now, it seemed to be nonsense. Indeed I thought so myself at the time. But I was wrong and I think you'll be convinced when you read my letter. Oh yes, and I told the Chairman you were in agreement.'

He gulped. 'Well, well, indeed, you may be right –'

'I am.'

He sat down abruptly and began fidgetting with a piece of paper, folding and unfolding, re-assessing the idea of a control group. Primitive people actually wanting not to be fed! Not to get into the benefit circle of PAX. Had they seen it like that? It was certainly possible to do so. If so the control group was valid. Anne clearly thought so, as someone on *Nature* must have done. So had he himself been stupid, not on his toes? Perhaps he had not been feeling well. Those interesting discoveries he had imagined! No, he certainly had not taken the boy's letter seriously. 'We have to think again' he muttered half to himself.

Yes, thought Anne, neither of us took it seriously, not at first. Odd, the immediate feeling she'd had when she read that letter from Rahul, that this was what Marie's warning could have been about: to be careful, why? Because of their economic involvement, that final and enormous profit? But not much, surely, from these aboriginals? Unless they were to be changed. Yes, that was partly what Rahul was on about. Or could Marie have been warning about their original contract with PAX? But could that be binding when the whole aim of the exercise was beginning to go wrong? Marie. Loyalty to Marie. Ah, that ... But is loyalty what love is about? No, nothing so dull, nothing so stupid, nothing so safe. She shook herself, wondered if she could have worded the letter more strongly. Probably not.

She and Saranjit, with some of the plant people from the lab settled down to make lists and to check, particularly, what had been done about the more poisonous of the leguminosae, not that many of them were free of marginally toxic elements, even good old peas and beans. Anne remembered her grandfather stopping her from eating laburnum seeds which she had picked for dinner in her play house. What could be more beautiful and apparently harmless than a gold tasseled laburnum? Perhaps a golden cassia? No, too big. Too many plants were too big. And as she took up another page of names: too many plants!

Now the director of sub-tropical cloning videoed up, anxious. What was happening? Were those shits on the Board blaming his crowd? Anne and Saranjit sympathized, told him what they knew and came up with further suggestions. Stop working along certain lines. Nothing wrong with the cereals nor, at present, the legumes. Here's the preliminary list of doubtfuls. Yes, nature seems to be having a bash at us. And by the way, Anne said, talking of *Nature*, there will be a letter in the next issue I'd like you to read.

'Anyway, Rahul will soon be coming over' she said comfortingly to Saranjit. His son!

'I shall first, I think, yes, first video Australia. I hope Ritchie will not bite!' said Saranjit. But there was no Ritchie, only Fred. 'So when will he be back?'

'We don't know. He's gone walkabout. Good old Australian habit, that is!'

'But where?'

'Well,' said Fred, 'we kind of think it could be Arnhem Land.'

'Now, what does that mean?' Saranjit asked, looking round. But Anne had no answer, only the wildest guesses. Only a feeling

135

of things drawing together.

Two days went by and there was no direct communication with the Board and only the official hand-outs, less than helpful. Reports were coming in now from Indonesia, South-East Asia, not so bad, but bad though, village people again the innocents. Two of the anti-morphogenesis groups had videoed but only one was abusive. The other was well informed with a couple of old friends on it. This was the one she had been talking to when the control group idea really took shape. But naturally they weren't to know this. Anne gave them what information she had, but it was all rather vague. They were waiting for accurate reports from the team which had flown out to the Pacific. So far their videos had been brief and sufficiently horrible. Clearly most people had died in great pain. For the moment the anti-Board group at the Centre was waiting.

It was noticeable that some of the news or comments about the virus or the storage conditions, none of them with much foundation in fact but providing some calming pseudo-science, was being crowded out in the cheaper media by a new type of entertainment in the early stage of its launching. Both Anne and Saranjit found it rather disgusting and both were fairly certain that it was one of the perhaps slightly illegitimate brain-children of Ideas, which of course meant PAX financing, direct or indirect. Saranjit only hoped his son hadn't had anything to do with it, but was afraid he might have and would even be proud of it.

Zeenat Jonsen flew in, visibly shaken, occasionally bringing in the Will of Allah, and discussed with them the bio-chemical relationships between the amino acids and the possibility of molecular crossings-over. They had a biggish staff meeting on this and possibilities were worked out and considered, but all the same a full range of improbabilities still seemed to exist.

'There are moments,' said Zeenat, 'when I wish the Board

had, instead, gone whole-heartedly for L.P. – leaf protein, you know, very simple, but not so – so pretty – as your plants, only the leaves were there already, ordinary unimproved leaves, but everywhere, everywhere!'

'Did they even consider it? Before our results were published?'

'I understand so,' said Zeenat, 'some time in the eighties or nineties, but they wanted total control and there was an obstinate old man, Pirie, who had started it all and he did not care for the Board. He did not appreciate the need for control in the interests of efficiency, something we all know now. No, it was to be done his way with very simple machinery that even ignorant village people could use. Oh, it wouldn't have been so efficient. Impossible. Nor would it have had such useful economic after-effects. But yet, perhaps he too could have fed many millions.'

'What an odd story,' said Saranjit, 'yes, I remember L.P. Pirie-Rothamsted, wasn't it? He came to India and tried to get it started. I was a young man, excited. I wanted them to go ahead. He had a little stammer I liked so much. I so wished to work with him – for India. But I was shy to ask. We may go back to it yet.'

'Very safe,' said Zeenat, 'but not exciting like yours. Not image-making. Ah, my dear Anne, my dear Saranjit, your beautiful gorgeous mathematics turning into marvellous plant forms, it was like a fairy tale. Like a kind of heaven. But perhaps we may, partially at least, have to come back to plain leaf protein.'

'Without the follow-up from the Board,' Anne said under her breath.

'But perhaps not. Perhaps all will go well. Sir Edmund is so confident – oh, wonderfully! Nothing is too much for him!' Not even all those deaths. Anne shook her head.

Zeenat left in a mixed mood, as did the others who came or videoed at length to consult, from genetics and from cloning, even from N.I.F. who were by this time much involved in

137

problems of suitable vegetation for projected space colonies, another interest which PAX was tentatively developing. Some felt that what had happened was only a temporary set-back, others that it meant total rethinking. The media hovered, were fed suitable scraps. But the anti-morphogenesis groups held meetings and published widely and often sensibly. They were turning people not only against Freefood, but against many other of the Board's activities. This might develop awkwardly indeed, though so far it could be played down. At the Centre there were Staff meetings and a go-slow on anything which could be slowed without damage. Between times Anne walked in the garden, briskly, impressing the young with her sudden new confidence. Her left arm was hurting again, she really must see a doctor. And then Rahul arrived suddenly, ran across the grass, gave her a huge hug and she forgot all about it again.

# CHAPTER TWENTY-ONE

There was the boardroom with its splendid wood and metal work, its pictures skilfully changed from time to time, though always with the great empty beautiful distance of the Fred Williams landscape where the Chairman could rest his eyes on it, with the maps and video-screens ready to set up at a touch, with the soft carpet and the Nobel citation. It was empty. Then Sir Edmund came in, with Ferguson, Marie-Claire Raffray and Bo Gustavsen the big Swede. Sad not to have Alberto, but he had retired to his vineyard and olive grove and what he called a cottage and grew unimproved fruit and vegetables. The main meeting would be – must be – later. They sat down, fidgetted, arranged their papers.

'We all understand what this is about,' said Ferguson, 'and we agree with you, Ed, that it is a serious situation. Very serious.'

'We have to come to our decision before the full Board meeting' Gustavsen said, 'that is a must.' There they were, so small a group, at one end of the long table.

'As you know,' said Sir Edmund, 'this is something completely unforeseen, which should never have happened. It leaves us somewhat unprepared, though never totally.'

'And we cannot say it is the direct fault of anyone,' said Marie-Claire, 'certainly not of the scientists at the Centre. All the tests had been run. Professor Ferguson and I flew over immediately and spoke at length to Anne Tomlin; she is, as you know, meticulous. I assured her that no possible blame attached to her or her immediate colleagues and staff. But – she was upset. Naturally.'

Sir Edmund noticed tears in her eyes and looked away. Somehow women always think first about individual people, not about the big effect! But Marie-Claire was essential liaison.

'Perhaps we tried too many plants' he said, half to himself, 'trying to please our public, our vast public. As was only correct. There seems to be nothing wrong with our original cereals.'

'It may have been a misjudgement to try the root crops, but all those islands wanting yams as well as taro! And the colocasias are good in some respects – and comparatively easy to work with, or so I hear from the geneticists.' That was Ferguson.

'Poor little Ethel Gabani, her people have suffered badly.' Marie-Claire again on an individual!

'We know,' said Sir Edmund, 'that an increase in the protein content had been effected. Say, in the taro. Could that have set up some other change?' He spoke with a little hesitation. His normal confidence had not quite extended to the genera.

'There was no sign of that, I understand' said Ferguson. 'There were also the dioscoreas, again spread over tropics and sub-tropics.'

'So what went wrong?'

'Dioscorin' muttered Gustavsen, who had been looking it up.

'We could have contained whatever went on over there – or so I believe' said Sir Edmund. 'No. It's the other thing that's going to be a trifle awkward. At our end.'

'The potatoes.' Nobody said anything immediately. They had certainly avoided any symptoms themselves, probably because they were all in the higher income group where potatoes played less part.

'We have been fortunate that there have been few deaths – so far, and these not totally attributable to solanine. We hope there will be no awkward side effects; however the symptoms are, I fear, typical. But –' Sir Edmund looked round, ' – do we compensate immediately or do we deny responsibility? It's a quite simple choice.' He had a few newspaper clippings in his hand; the others had seen them. The Board had not, so far, been under direct attack, but in some quarters Freefood was being blamed, though possibly the conditions of storage or of transport. But that had been so carefully gone into three seasons ago! Their own newspapers and video channels had carried the news but for the time being put the blame onto an entirely new virus, perhaps even an escape from one of the space probes.

'Essential not to have a public enquiry,' said Ferguson. 'The wrong people would be sure to get on it.'

'That's right,' said the Swede heavily, 'And keep off compensation. Nothing has been proved against us and with the numbers involved in the Pacific area, it would be – an intolerable drain on our resources. On the shareholders.'

Sir Edmund nodded agreement; he had been into the figures. Gustavsen went on: 'Do we know at all how it happened? At what point?'

'I think I have the story,' said Marie-Claire, 'from Anne. She explained how they had worked on the cereals, including rice and millet for the tropics, also on fruits and, latterly, legumes, but you were keen that any group of peole could have its choice, Edmund –'

'Scarcely myself. The Board.'

She smiled. 'If you like to put it that way, Edmund. But perhaps the whole world could only be fed so in our great plan, in our hopes from which we started. Well now, there was some crossing done with the dioscoreas, the yams. These I must remind you, all contain small traces of dioscorin. No, Edmund, the one they call yam in America is something else, you need have no anxiety. This crossing was intended to improve the protein content which is low in some – Zeenat would tell you – in fact she was not very keen on yams. There was also work done on the aroids which, of course, include the taro and the so-called elephant yam. We realized that the people who normally eat these root crops always get out the poison by washing and boiling –'

'Do you mean that taro can be poisonous? We have sent in so much –'

'No, Gustav. Taro only has calcium oxalate. Unwholesome but not a quick killer, not like dioscorin. If only poor dear Ethel's people had been taking that but unfortunately they liked the yams better. They seem to have fitted in with a cargo-cult suggestion and been specially welcomed. All these root and stem crops need treatment. This includes the euphorbias, cassava, tapioca. You may remember the suggestion that work should be done on them? Fortunately – yes, by good fortune – it had not been started.' She looked across at the Chairman. Had he winced a little? Or was she only imagining it?

'Surely taro is safe! Nasty stuff that it is.'

'Not if it is what you like. And it appears that the consumers have continued with their normal practice, time wasting as we may think it. Yes, the women went on. Luckily. You understand –' She looked round at the three men. '– I learned this from Anne – that almost all edible plants have some small amount of poison in them somewhere, usually so little as to be harmless, but sometimes – not. Those who normally eat these plants know how to deal with the poisons, often by a well-known cooking technique; for instance, we do not eat raw potatoes. Why? Because people hundreds – no, thousands, of years ago – found that they were only wholesome if they were cooked. There is no reason to suppose those in the Pacific islands have changed their methods. But if by some misfortune the dosage of poisonous substance is suddenly – say, tripled – well, you can imagine!'

'They should have tested!' said Gustavsen.

'They did test – rigorously. But something seems to have gone wrong during the cloning process and possibly at a late stage. It might conceivably even, have developed after distribution. The deaths are due either to massive doses of calcium oxalate in the improved taro or, more probably, to dioscorin in another yam which was a cross . . .'

Ferguson interrupted. 'But, my dear Marie-Claire, surely there must have been some sign in the laboratory-manipulated plant?'

'No,' she said, 'Anne Tomlin was definite. All possible checks had been made. Neither she nor Saranjit Singh can imagine what exactly went wrong. Routine checks were made during cloning; nothing appeared. There is a theory – but –'

'Does it or does it not make us responsible?'

'Now, Ed, is this the right approach?' Suddenly they found themselves all talking at once: 'We have to keep the whole Board informed –' 'Our duty –' 'All stocks must be destroyed.' 'We have to stand together –' 'Even if there had been one, just one, terrible mistake, Freefood is what matters – feeding the whole world –'

But at the end from Sir Edmund: 'All stocks of root food have been called in, whether or not there have been any unfortunate occurrences, and are being replaced by cereals. When available, there has been some replacement of edible roots from pre-Freefood stock. For instance, some of the speciality potatoes which certain restaurants keep in supply. But most consumers tend to find this unsatisfactory. They don't cook so evenly; there may even be small blemishes or discolouration. People have got used to our standards of – well, perfection. In the media, blame has been placed as far as possible on methods of storage.'

'Or this virus story? Too far-out perhaps?'

'Our Ideas people are at work. As to compensation, we are determined that there will be no individual compensation, but where an isolated population has been almost completely wiped out, sad as this is, we shall rehabilitate, rebuild, make a show place, perhaps a hospital, an institute – do you agree?' He turned to Marie-Claire: 'We do not intend in any way to blame the scientists, at any rate as things appear at present. And we shall take all possible steps to stop this happening elsewhere. Further we shall ensure that there is no talk of it happening again. You know how prone certain groups are to do this.' Yes, they all knew.

Professor Ferguson said tentatively: 'There are probably considerable amounts of the original roots in many parts of the tropics – taro, cassava – which appear to be unaltered. They could presumably be found, paid for if in private hands, and distributed.'

'I hardly think so,' said Sir Edmund, 'remember, it is against our policy to supply anything outside our own excellent lines. We made a small concession over potatoes, but definitely not cassava or yams. No.' He pushed back his chair. They were all curiously exhausted. Or was it curious?

Yes, this was clearly the correct attitude. But one other thing occurred to Professor Ferguson. He coughed gently: 'By the way, Edmund, about that letter which Anne Tomlin wrote to *Nature*: that can, I trust, be disregarded? We don't want that on the top of – this.'

'Unfortunately,' said the Chairman, 'they appear to be going to print it. But I have alerted a couple of good names who will point out the obvious problems and difficulties. I think this too can be contained. Yes, I have no doubt. And, I trust, it can be done without unduly affecting our relationship with the Centre.' He glanced at Marie-Claire, but she did not look back at him; her lips were a little tight. Yes, he thought, she is beginning to show her age.

It was Gustavsen who started up the discussion on the anti-morphogenesis groups. Clearly the Chairman had hoped to avoid this for the moment, but Ferguson as well had things he wanted to say. Marie-Claire did not join in but listened with care. There was more to think about. During the discussion on the anti-morphogenesis groups some interesting and unexpected names were coming up. She made notes quietly. Things began to take shape in her mind, set off by a phrase in Anne's letter about control groups being necessarily less interested in imported trivialities. If the Chairman thought he could contain Anne's letter to *Nature*, he was wrong. He might also be wrong if he supposed it would be permanently possible to keep the links between PAX and the Corporation out of the public eye. Nothing had been totally hidden but, as far as the Board was concerned, not all

144

wanted to look. Investigative journalism can probably be contained (nice hygienic word!). What, after all, are lawyers for? But not *Nature*, not so easily.

She herself knew about the Corporation, not everything, but sufficient. Undermining the Chairman? Of course. She would not even tell Anne! Possible, for example, that a small liaison group could be formed between some of these names in her notes and perhaps some of the newer members of the Board who had not been completely swallowed up by the PAX ambience. That bright young West Indian? Perhaps Ethel Gabani herself, perhaps Alberto if she could wake him up. Schulman? No. To arrive at what Freefood ought to be: how people could be fed without being corrupted. A simple idea really. But not for the health of the Corporation in which, indeed, she held shares. But to hell with that. As Anne would undoubtedly say.

For a moment she thought in terms of dance, when the music changes subtly and the Prima Ballerina – herself? Anne? – breaks into a solo of shattering brilliance. But no, no. And poor Bobbo dead for so long, but had left her his fortune which he had forgotten to spend and the name which was not even his own. Ah well! She switched to careful attention and note-taking.

And after it was all worked out and in action she would go back and tell Anne, and how she would laugh!

A few more decisions were made or those the Chairman had already set in motion agreed to. It was agreed that during the next few days there would be two or three more informal meetings, much like this one, with some of the more important and knowledgable members, sometimes with new ideas or information.

At one of these Dr Ikewa sat quietly for some time taking notes on the discussion about the Pacific disaster which had also hit some of the Japanese smaller islands, either through yams or

145

perhaps taro. Yes, a few deaths: farmers and small fishermen. It was just as well, he thought, that so far there had been no suggestion of modification of any of the edible sea-weeds. Had there been a mistake there, what a trouble! However, he had himself seen to it that preliminary analysis should be done in the laboratory founded by his own ex-group, which would ensure that if such a project were to be considered at some later date, it would be certain to go to them. Dr Ikewa still had strong familial feelings towards his ex-group even though they had pressed him to accept the Board's invitation to join.

The discussion moved on again to the increasing seriousness of the anti-morphogenesis bodies and the other critics (some for reasons which appeared to him as ludicrous) of PAX policies. Much of this could be discounted or channelled in other directions, but not all. There had been a worthwhile memorandum from Ideas. Perhaps it was inevitable, and must be set against the undoubted gratitude of countless millions who had been rescued from semi-starvation, including those who had found their local dictatorships had been more effectively undermined and often replaced from rather more amiable sources, by PAX organization and results than by earlier revolutions. Troubles had come, in general, not from the previously under-developed countries, but from nearer home. 'Could be,' said Bo Gustavsen, 'we should pull out. Not too much. But showing. In Europe maybe. Or the U.S.A. Concentrate elsewhere.'

'Amongst those who appreciate us,' said Ferguson.

'The less developed, who will build us into their culture patterns permanently,' added Dr Schulman.

When the discussion had simmered down, Dr Ikewa rose, bowed politely and suggested that perhaps the time had also come to consider just how the Board itself had been reacting to social criticism of its policy. Was it not possible that there was too

146

much division of opinion, perhaps too much attention paid to what, after all, was merely uninformed shoutings and mutterings from sources who could not take in solid realities? He went on: 'As I am sure you know, gentlemen, that is to say ladies and gentlemen, we have in Japan for very many centuries enjoyed a system of – Houses in which the Head or Director is totally responsible for all below him. It is for him to make sure that all goes well in his great household. Down to the least. He orders gifts for the children of his subordinates. For their wives. He sees that marriages and funerals are conducted in such a way as will credit not merely the relatives, but the company – the House, his great family. He does this through those below him. In return he receives total order and loyalty. As due to a father. He receives birthday greetings from all. All.' Dr Ikewa noticed that the Chairman was looking a trifle uneasy. But why? For honour of Japan he must give necessary information! He went on: 'In another House it is the same. And this shining and noble House may be a company. Or a University. Or, in a sense, a political party. A research laboratory. People thinking in the same direction. Is it not a little sad that our PAX is not such a House?'

A certain unusual silence followed. Good? Bad? Dr Schulman felt a quick surge of feminism and refrained from useless comment of the kind which had sprung to her lips. Bo Gustavsen muttered: 'Birthday greetings!' Professor Ferguson was doodling away. 'An interesting thought,' said Sir Edmund, 'but, as you say, Dr Ikewa, the Japanese system has centuries of history behind it. I doubt whether it would fit in with the western concepts of democracy on which PAX is based.'

'No?' said Dr Ikewa sadly. It had seemed so obvious to him, so clean a way out of pointless talk and division. And his own loyalties could have been sublimated, for they still chafed him. He could have removed himself totally with scarcely any residual

147

traumas to the House of the Chairman, to be all that was required of him. He had accepted this when his name was put forward as a Board member. His ancestors had been Samurai, poor Samurai no doubt, but bright-sworded. He still had his sword. Here and there eyes avoided him. He tried once more: 'I hear that there is trouble in Australia, among the very poor and ignorant who should be among the foremost in appreciating the Freefood.'

'That is so,' said Sir Edmund. 'Our organization has not been entirely accepted. It will perhaps be a matter of time and persuasion.'

'Our own primitives were also unwilling at first' said Dr Ikewa eagerly. 'But we took measures. Firm leadership is necessary. Should you wish for consultation, we would be altogether happy.'

'Thank you, Dr Ikewa,' said Sir Edmund, 'but we are fully in touch with Darwin.'

Dr Ikewa sat down, saddened. Dr Schulman and Marie-Claire glanced at one another, the tiniest eyebrow lift. Bo Gustavsen breathed like a surfacing hippo. And suddenly the name of that place, Darwin, came alive to Dr Ikewa. It was the town over which the plane had been shot down during the invasion of Australia in his great grandfather's time. And if the invasion had been successful, if we had won that war, Dr Ikewa thought, there would not be any trouble with the primitives. Oddly enough, the same thought had whisked through the mind of one or two of the other Board members.

Another meeting discussed the notions which had come up from Ideas, discarding most of them. Finally, there were figures to be gone into: everyone must be made to understand. The Chairman was patient. Yet so much was marginal. At the back of it all was the dark curtain: death walking across their well illuminated path. Making uncertainties, revisions, shifting the balance of

148

importances. And again, that letter from Anne Tomlin, which showed – yes, definitely showed – that she and perhaps others of the scientists who had been so dependable, were no longer totally behind the Board. And if there was a crack there it was perhaps even more serious than the Pacific deaths.

But then came the full Board meeting, the long table filled. Members had arrived in various states of anxiety and agitation, but it was immediately calming to find that the Chairman's confidence was unshaken. It was good to hear with such certainty that the trouble could be contained, that there would be no further cause for anxiety, that what had happened was one of the dreadful accidents outside of human control: an act, as they used to say, of God. If the Board had any direct responsibility it was through having tried to meet the tastes and wishes of people who had never used cereals or legumes as a basic food. Yet this was true democracy. 'We have never,' said Sir Edmund, 'and it is something the Board should be proud of, put pressure on any group to conform to other people's eating habits.' That had a noble sound, quotable, in fact, an ethical decision. But Ethel Gabani, who had seen too many deaths – dioscorin results in total paralysis of the nervous system – cried quietly in spite of the anti-depressants which Dr Schulman, also concerned, had persuaded her to take. These women!

Those members who spoke all agreed on one point; it was essential that nothing should appear which might be used, at least effectively, by any of the anti-morphogenesis groups. It was more than fortunate that so few deaths had been directly attributable to solanine from the potatoes. But this was because they were, nowadays, not an entire staple food anywhere. If this had happened in Ireland eight generations back – !

'Where else might poisoning of some sort crop up?' asked one member. But Sir Edmund answered: 'We hope and trust, nowhere. Our aim is to continue, as we have done, to feed the world.' Nothing was mentioned at this meeting about the Australian problem. But it was probably not important, affecting, what? – half a million people at most.

In the end the Board meeting broke up with the feeling that all would be well if everyone stuck together, a warm, wartime feeling. Even Ethel Gabani was a little comforted, as a survivor after a stricken field whose dead would be avenged.

# CHAPTER TWENTY-TWO

'Look, my son,' said Saranjit, 'you are telling us that Neil Ritchie is accepted among those people of yours and actually, you say, agreeing and helping. After all that wheat! After all that rudeness. That – that dirt talk.'

'I think, somehow, they were linked,' Rahul said. 'He liked the challenges but he never cared for the actualities, especially the large machines. He never liked heavy technology. It stopped the – the intuitive answer to the challenge. He only put up with delicate things. Like mathematics, some kinds. He has plenty of challenges now.'

Anne and Saranjit looked at one another. 'If – if what you say is anywhere near being scientific truth!'

Rahul smiled at his father: 'I have been describing what I experienced and what I lived through, and I have tried to trace back calmly for possible origins in pre-history. I have also tried to trace forward as far as rationally possible.'

'But I still cannot see Neil Ritchie there among your savages!'

'You see, father, it is all because he is an intuitive, in all his work perhaps – all his thinking. It is a little like good cooking, no use reading it in the books. My mother would tell you that! Does she know I am back?'

'Cooking, cooking! – what is intuitive about Ritchie's work?'

'He sees things, smells, tastes. Sometimes he measures. And it all comes together deep down in his mind so that he can make deductions. He uses sense extensions, the microscope for instance, but he is a little bit ambivalent about some mathematics – your kind of mathematics, dear Anne. I never quite understood why, for he uses it as – as a tool, but he won't let it interfere with his intuitions, and sometimes they don't seem to have a logical base, but that is because they are far too deep.'

Saranjit shook his head. 'And is that why – ' Anne hesitated 'why he gets on with your black friends?'

'And white. And coffee colour. But all with – well, a background of intuitive knowledge. Which Ritchie latches onto.'

Anne looked at him hard.

'Yes,' he said, 'as I do myself.'

The other two looked at one another. Did this mean anything? Had Rahul slipped away from the scientific point of view? Anne poured another cup of coffee all round. How well Rahul was looking, stronger, more grown-up and yet with the same delightful young freshness.

'You speak,' she said, 'as if your Aboriginals were always, well, sensible and peaceful. Where do their normal aggressions go?'

'Ah,' he said, 'That's something those psychologists keep telling us about. Normal aggressions. But my people didn't have to have them. There was plenty of room. Their enemies were weather and rocks and it's no use being aggressive with them.'

'Come, come,' said Anne, 'don't tell me they didn't murder white settlers and explorers.'

'Of course they did, or tried to, rather inefficiently. They hadn't had enough practice. They were angry because they were hurt. That's not aggression. Listen Anne! The white invaders were interfering deeply with basic relationships, with their whole lives. Squatters and graziers brought in those huge mobs of sheep and cattle which ate up all the vegetation. They ate all the desert and semi-desert species which had adapted over untold centuries but could so easily be wiped out forever. They let their sheep graze off the seeding annual grasses and wondered that they never came up again! They made deserts. That was what civilization did.' He looked to see if his father and Anne were taking this in.

Anne nodded agreement. This was the way more than one desert had started. Nobody learns! This was beginning to be so interesting that she could forget the deaths and disown feelings of responsibility and blame, at least for a time. Rahul went on: 'There wasn't enough left for the grazing animals with whom my people had had before this a food relationship; the kangaroos and euros and wallabies and, oh, the little ones. Birds too! People had fed well in the old days, moving about. They didn't starve till their world was spoiled. On top of that the miners came and tore up the ground, the mother of everything, and after tearing they left it ruined, violated, covered with dirty remains, broken bottles and tins and rags. There they lie still along the old mine tracks! And bits of useless metal and crockery and jags of wood. Who wouldn't try to rid their country, their home, of this horror? When Pigeon, the tracker, was sent to catch Ellemara, the cattle killer, he did it, but Ellemara showed him that the real enemy was the white man. So those two and their friends waged a small war, but were so easily overcome and killed. Others killed

152

too. Vengeance! That was only four or five generations back in the north-west where now there are so few left. Countless others dead, always ten of them killed for one white! The women were taken and swapped about, girls like Naburdja, like she must look when she goes back to camp. And the Missions took the children away from their mothers so as to bring them up as servants, as slaves almost. Oh dear, I talk and talk but it didn't happen to me.'

'So now,' said Anne, 'you say they are living in good relationship with their natural environment, not changing it? How on earth does Ritchie fit in? Or you yourself, Rahul? And what about the Freefood?'

'Well, it's possible to alter your relationship with the eco-system, if you want to, like you can with your parents, but gently, so as to keep the good part. You see, they don't have mobs of sheep or cattle, but they do have a few horses, because you can talk to horses, and some of the families who farm, mostly part white, have a few milking cows and – you'll laugh perhaps – artificial insemination. The little planes bring it from a centre. Oh yes! About the planes and the landrovers: it's well known that the men on the coastal oil wells get dangerously out of touch, so they swap round and when they come out they're made much of as if – as if they'd escaped from a giant. They never stay beyond half a year and when they go back they have been strengthened to do it again for the sake of their country.

'There is a good deal of simple solar energy used; it makes sense there. It's possible, you see, to have controlled technology, a fire inside a hearth, not burning the house down.'

'That has never happened yet. It does not seem – genuinely possible.' Saranjit was doubtful. 'People start simply, then they begin to want things. They have to buy them – with something. Or else the things are given – at a price.'

'Which is their souls. Their inner existence. Their way back into

153

intuitive knowledge. Which perhaps you do not think you believe in, father! Too big a price. My friends in Australia are not paying it.'

'Are you sure they are not going to?'

'Ritchie will help with certain reasonable wants. To make the water serve the land better. Now there is too much or too little. He has ideas about this. He has, let's say, intuitions. How things can be done without destroying what cannot be replaced. When I go back . . . '

'You intend to go back?'

'Of course, dear Anne, dear father. When we have quite stopped this Freefood nonsense. But you will have to help me. This letter to *Nature* is good as a beginning, but perhaps the Board will not accept it. Let us agree to begin with that my country, Murngin, is a control area. The Board can swallow that. But really it is more, much more. It is a new way of thinking about food. Quickly that becomes a new way of thinking about the natural world. It is an enormous idea which could, itself, spread, developing its own science. I think not everyone likes Freefood; there must be other control areas, as they could be called for a face-save. You see?'

'I see' said Anne and looked across at Saranjit. But it was possible that the Board would not accept the idea of control areas. And if so? Then the old amah came in with a plate heaped with lovely, bright-coloured sweets decorated with the thinnest gold and silver tissues, as for a king – or the chairman of a board. 'Your mother welcomes her son,' said the amah.

'Ah,' said Rahul, picking one up, 'Not Freefood, I see!' and to the amah: 'Tell her I am coming, almost at once!' He licked his finger, then said to Anne: 'Now, how about drafting a letter to the Board and get this settled while I'm with my mother? Quite a different letter from the one to *Nature* which, you tell me, has not convinced them. A harder letter!' He grinned at her, then was off to his mother and doubtless more goodies.

'I'll try' said Anne. She felt her heart pounding with excitement and began to suck one of the sweets. Yes, too right, definitely not Freefood! 'I'll type this myself,' she said, plugged in her favourite old typewriter and put in a carbon. She smiled at what she was doing. Old-fashioned no doubt, but there was a definite job-satisfaction about it. Occasionally she looked up at the wall opposite and one of the original much blown-up micro-photographs of a new type chloroplast. She nodded at it, an old friend. Saranjit, who of course had never typed a line himself, watched, often making his usual protests. 'I think I'll start with convincing Marie.'

'Ah' he said, 'you may be right. That could open the door. If you do convince her – but are we convinced ourselves? Are we mad?'

'Mad, yes. But I'm willing to have a go,' she said, crossed out a word with fierce Xes and put in another. 'Doing things their way has gone wrong. We'll try again.'

'Yes' he said, 'this is different. Other words. Other ideas. Perhaps we are too old. Yet we were most unhappy, both you and I, yes. And now my son brings hope.'

She went on typing, sometimes laughing a little to herself, muttering 'She'll see what I mean,' and then 'Oh, trust Marie to guess what's coming!'

'If this comes off,' said Saranjit, 'we might even be able to help these – savages that Rahul believes in, perhaps improving some of their native plants, not too much. So that they could do everything themselves, in their own way, with their own kind of worship. For that must be what it is.'

'Yes,' she said, 'Perhaps that's how to put it. Oh, it could be fun!' She slipped in another sheet, was now slowing down, the

155

first draft almost finished. She had been so tense, her arm ached, her chest. And suddenly the pain in her arm and right across her body increased, enveloped her totally, an enormous wave breaking over her. And then retreating, was gone. No pain. And Anne was dead. Saranjit caught her as she began to topple off her chair, held her in his arms, thinking stupidly that this was the first time he had done so, laid her on the cushions, shouted for help, but knew it would be useless.

# CHAPTER TWENTY-THREE

The memorandum from Saranjit Singh, accompanied by parts of the letter from Anne Tomlin, had been circulated. But the letter itself had been sent, as was intended, only to Marie-Claire Raffray. Sir Edmund understood that.

'I knew,' he said gently, to her alone, 'yes, indeed I knew that you had a particular friendship with our earliest scientific colleague, Anne Tomlin, for whom of course I had the deepest respect.' He looked round the table, speaking in his normal voice – 'Her scientific integrity ... deeply mourned . . all the Board join me ... ' But Marie-Claire was not listening. Instead she listened inwardly to Anne, to Anne's voice going soft. More than five years. And now it was over and she herself, she might as well grow old and die. But her letter, her last letter unsigned, and Saranjit sending it on with a cold note. Cruelly. No, perhaps not, for by then she knew. The Board had been told, the meeting quickly convened. The letter, the letter. The little misspellings, as always. She kept thinking of them, of Anne's fingers on the type writer, not of the letter's content. As she should, she must think of it and come to a decision, for herself and perhaps for the Board.

Sir Edmund was going on: 'The defection of Dr Ritchie – I can only, at present, call it that – is one of the most astonishing features. With his record of success in implementing our ideas! But you were saying, my dear Ferguson?'

Professor Ferguson said: 'This cable from Darwin: clearly they think he has been abducted, want to know if we would authorize an expedition – '

'With gunboats!' This giggle was from a very recent Board member, a highly cultivated young man from Barbados. 'And perhaps armed camels!'

'I think not,' said Sir Edmund, 'only civil servants. Of whom there are a peculiar abundance in Darwin. We need pay no attention.'

Ferguson was annoyed, but the tension had been broken. Marie-Claire could begin to think about Anne's message to her. But she had passed it on, yes, she had done that! Anne would have meant her to, had probably intended a more formal statement to the Board. But that had been written, not by her but by Saranjit Singh alone. The last to be with her. She listened now. It appeared that the Board were not all of one mind, so how would it go? Must she intervene? The Chairman had not given a clear lead, but was explaining the latest developments. The big outbreaks among the root crops had been contained. The general outcry had died down or been deflected. Would agreement in principle to the idea of a control group break the unity of Board policy? Suddenly Ethel Gabani gave a little cough and said in a

157

small voice: 'My people demand to discontinue the Freefood. I am sorry, but they are united on this. Very united.' And then she added in a louder voice: 'Those who survive.'

'Dear me' said Sir Edmund, genuinely taken aback, 'I too am sorry, Miss Gabani. We had sent two consignments of mixed cereals, two large plane loads.'

'I am so sorry,' she said again, 'but they made a big fire and – and – it has all been destroyed. They said it was – wrong cargo. People still have gardens – and the old things.'

'I see,' said Sir Edmund. 'Well, we cannot use force. We can only hope that in time, this dreadful accident will be forgotten, and should they change their minds, we shall immediately come in again.'

And then a newish political Board member who had never, as far as anyone remembered, said anything but yes or please in a thick accent, or agreed silently, stood up. He was wearing a very remarkable shirt and before he spoke he took out of its front a kind of hat with black and white tails and put it on. 'We don't like Freefood,' he said. 'Going back to lookoo.' He sat down and nobody had any idea what he (or they) could be going back to. Animal or vegetable? Another control area; yet another! The Charman passed back a quick note and a whisper. And Marie-Claire was thinking to herself, never again, never, never. Cherie. My Anne. So much better not to be the one who survives.

Professor Ferguson spoke: 'Surely we must not act pre-cipitately. No doubt we are all feeling the shock of our most esteemed colleague's death, but it should not deflect us from the policy which was jointly, and, if I may say so, wisely agreed upon, only a short time ago.'

The Chairman did not move, but several members gave signs of approval. However it was Bo Gustavsen who spoke: 'Policy is that thing we can change. I have been home, also in video. It

158

appears that the anti-morphogenesis movement is no longer just a few, what you call, cranks, but even a big scientific opinion.' He mentioned two names which made the Board sit up. Even the Chairman frowned and pencilled a note. 'There is this group in Sweden and a sister group in Denmark who are not taking the Freefood. I do not think we can disregard.'

'Perhaps it will die down,' Ferguson said, 'as the American groups did.'

'No,' said Gustavsen. 'It is policy that has to alter. This is a must.'

Sir Edmund spoke: 'Of course we have never attempted to use force. Even when it was justified. You may remember the affair when our two senior agents, poor chaps, got into – trouble – in the opium country. No, no, we must meet our dissidents and talk it over, quietly. After all, we must not forget that they consume at least an average amount of our other commodities. So, compromise, when necessary. Compromise is all. Do you agree, ladies and gentlemen?' There was a general murmur of assent. 'What a pity our old friend Alberto is not here,' the Chairman went on, 'he has gathered quite a village of peasants and, I suppose we might call them, intellectuals, round his charming Italian estate. They have excellent fruit and vegetables and are developing a really superb liqueur. But they also take an almost average amount of Freefood.'

'I heard from dear old Al,' said Dr Schulman, 'that it was just great for fattening the village hogs.' There was an easing of laughter round the table.

'So is our future policy to be in general one of relaxing?' the Chairman asked, leaning forward, looking round, gathering assent, though not yet from all members. But gathered nothing either way from Marie-Claire Raffray, nothing but grief.

'What I don't get' the Barbadian said suddenly, 'is how this –

159

well, this allowing of what you like to call control areas will affect our shareholders. Their share of the bread.'

'Bread?' asked Dr Ikewa.

'Money' the Barbadian snapped back, irritated. So, thought Ikewa, bread is cash: nice.

The Chairman went on, frowning a little: 'I doubt if this dissent has the significance that we recently assumed. Indeed I did so myself. But fluency of method is essential. Mr Gustavsen agrees with me.' Bo nodded forcefully. 'After all, PAX is not solely devoted to the Freefood aspect of its activity – not today, although at the beginning it had deep importance. As you will, most of you, recollect.' He gestured at the Nobel citation. 'What is perhaps of greater import to our shareholders and ourselves is the follow-up of economic activity which resulted when hitherto marginally hungry populations were fed. This has been extremely successful and shows no signs of decrease.' He looked at the Barbadian. 'Employment is definitely picking up. Our aim, therefore, should be to continue supplying Freefood in all areas where the basic need exists, or shall we say, existed before we came on to the scene, which is to say most of the millions of our world population, so that our shareholders need have no anxiety about their . . . bread. But our policy will be to put absolutely no pressure on any community which does not wish to accept it. They will, naturally, share in the general economic activity and will probably take an increasing interest as the space programme progresses. There will be a certain degree of cutting down on the scientific staff, but perhaps that can be spaced out.'

'I can't see our antis going on after that' said Dr Schulman, satisfied.

Marie-Claire spoke in a low voice: 'If we accept the principle of control groups, as I think we should, following this – this memorandum from – from the Centre, we shall need observers.'

160

'Of whom, presumably, Neil Ritchie is already one' Sir Edmund said.

'If he can be so considered,' said Ferguson, 'but he may be in some peculiar way involved. Brain-washed. If you recollect, his grandparents were from Oban: west coast. Not hard-headed, apt to believe – too much. All those songs. Fairies.'

'Come, come, Professor Ferguson,' said Sir Edmund, 'his semi-desalination plants are sufficiently hard-headed in design.' Ferguson grunted. Suddenly Marie-Claire found she hated her colleagues on the Board. Except Ethel Gabani, who still bore the marks of pain. But especially the Chairman. Who had won. As he always did. Or seemed to have won, made it appear that he had won.

Anne was never like that. She wasn't interested in winning, only in doing something worth doing in her own, strict terms of worth. And being light-hearted with it, as perhaps good people mostly are. Yes, she'd enjoyed being attracted by other women and attracting them, just for fun. But she always came back to me. Until now. When she'd rushed off to do what she knew was worth doing, leaving me. And she won't come back. Not to me, not ever.

So I have to go on, as I did when I made my first contacts with the Antis. It would mean that control groups were not just moves in the power game. They would begin to be something different in kind. As Anne had known. Anne. For a moment she stared at the surface of the table, the papers, the rich reflections of the board room, heard voices congratulating the Chairman on a successful meeting, noticed that the Barbadian was frowning. He will be interested to hear where most of the bread goes. Yes, I shall get him. And if I fail? Edmund would certainly revenge himself. Somehow, I'd be off the Board. But I wouldn't care, not now.

There was shuffling of papers. Some rose. She avoided Ferguson whose condolences would have been unbearable. She spoke to her next contact. 'Ethel' she said, 'I want to have a word with you.' It was going to be a very interesting time. But not fun any more. Because when we have worked it, when we have shown up Edmund's PAX as the cover-up it is, I will not be able to tell Anne.

# CHAPTER TWENTY-FOUR

'Show me,' said Neil Ritchie, 'once more. Yes, Now –'

'Now you' said Djiuvalji. 'Good. Very near. You learn quick. Better than most part-white. I think you look first with outside eyes, but with inside eyes after: and better.'

'Maybe.' He looked critically at the throwing stick. Could it be improved? Or not?

'You think that sounds mad? No?' He was watching Neil very carefully.

'Mad? Oh no. It's quite clear. Hope it goes on working. Some days I manage it, some days not. Can't tell. Not yet.'

'Soon you do it every day. Easy. You like it here? Truly?'

'Wouldn't stay on if I didn't. It's not liking so much as learning.'

'We learn too. We learn from you. This thing about changing. The look-at measuring. The little hills that move.' He waved his fingers expressively.

'Graphs.'

'Yes, yes, I like them.' Djiuvalji danced a little at the pleasure of graphs. 'I can't see school figures. Tables they made me learn – tried to! This multiplying and dividing in books. Never could. No. But yours I can hold in my mind. I can make them grow – meet.'

'You'll need them for water planning. If you can hold them, all together and each separate, like a bundle of spears, you won't have to bother about arithmetic. I don't care for it myself.' He said nothing for a moment, then 'I think someone is trying to call me.' He shut his eyes, sinking deeper.

Djiuvalji tiptoed away. He said to Monju, one of the other men: 'That one learns so quick. He can feel spirits. He can move between worlds. He is altogether a snake.'

Monju agreed, remembering how quickly this man had learned to throw a spear. How his hand, by itself, took the right grasp on the womera: 'Perhaps once he was one of us. Do you think that?'

'That could be. But now he is listening. Listening, from inside. Look! He says that he is being called. Get the horses.'

Rahul had come back to the Institute at Darwin. He was feeling deeply shaken, but was determined not to show it, instead to be the complete scientist, as Anne would have wanted. He had rather a mixed reception. There were conformists who pointed to the necessity of modernizing this state within a state. And why, after all, had the Northern Territory been made into an Australian state except for the good of the Aboriginal population? A few dissenting sniggers here, but the conformists swept them aside. Look at the health department already growing out of its ample offices, and its main job to clear up on infant mortality, clinics and innoculations, special care for the aged and so on. And of course it was urgent to modernize oil production on the coast which was not being properly exploited in the general interest and would not be so long as it was left in aboriginal control. Look how they have been hampering the mining operations ever since the beginning! At the Institute there was, certainly, some criticism of the public servants; more should be left to nutritionists and ecologists. They added that there were some aboriginal practices which could surely not be allowed. Had Rahul heared about – ? But he had and it did not worry him. He thought briefly of Naburdja and smiled.

On the other hand, there was a group at the Institute which was delighted at the whole concept of a control area, to be carefully monitored for the effects of refusing the Freefood. They wondered how it had got past the Board, and Rahul gave them his version of what he assumed had happened. Who knows what goes on in the mind of others, even the closest? Yet, it was possible to know just that. Rahul had begun to learn how to do it, from others who were more advanced, but this was not something to mention at a place like the Institute. Later on perhaps. Or perhaps not. Certainly this was not the moment to discuss the business of picking up what was in fact going on underneath from those who were willing and in a position to co-operate. He himself was still far from certainty. He was hoping soon to see Naburdja again; she might have something to tell him about – about Anne. So lost he was, wanting to hold on, wanting to learn. Was it possible that Neil Ritchie could be learning too? Suddenly, in the middle of a conversation and a glass of Institute orange juice, he began reaching towards Neil.

He assured the nutritionists that there was plenty to eat among the aboriginals in their country. It was quite possible to adjust to temporary gaps, to something under the daily normal intake, especially of dairy fats and sugars, as the same people adjusted to feasts also. Babies looked fine and he thought the population was going up, quite apart from the in-gathering which, as they knew, was taking place all over Australia. Yes, there were schools, including technical education of an impressive standard, but people understood things especially mathematics in other ways; the frame of reference was different. He did not think that Australian-type examinations would produce results which could be considered in any way relevant. And now, he said, he must go off to the gate where he would be picked up.

'Have you told them?'

'They will know.'

His colleagues at the Institute raised eye-brows, but he seemed positive. Well, one of the Institute trucks would take him that far.

Neil Ritchie was there, not without problems connected with the wet. But there is nothing which cannot with intelligence and good will and above all understanding of what it really is, be deflected into a helpful relationship with people. So long as people don't demand too much too quickly. 'Tell me about Anne Tomlin' Neil said.

Rahul grimaced, bit his lip. 'They scattered her ashes,' he said. 'At least – the ashes of her body.'

'A pity she never got here,' said Neil. 'She'd have been interested. Or wouldn't she?'

'I – I think so,' Rahul answered, finding himself rather incapable of speaking calmly and sensibly about Anne. He swallowed and went on: 'There's to be a memorial meeting in London. She still has – had – some relatives in England. The Board is arranging it.'

'Fuck the Board,' said Neil.

'I suppose there'll be speeches and all that. Expensive music.'

'They'll turn it into a PAX occasion. Trust them! I can bloody see it. Need you go?'

'I'll have to be there because of my father. He will, you know, want me by him.'

'Good enough, mate. But look, is it dead sure we here can go on, not taking the Freefood nor any other bloody thing of theirs we don't want? Fair dinkum?'

'My father has said so,' said Rahul. 'We are Sikhs. They have agreed. They dare not do otherwise. But there is something else. We have here, and I am certain of this, a working set of relationships, of harmonies which the rest of the world has never had, partly because we out there started badly, fighting sabretooth tigers and mammoths – and one another. But the other way could be learned. If you and I can learn it, so can others.

'Right,' said Neil, 'and nothing to it once you can stop believing what the rest tell you. The Institute mob for instance. Darwin!' He spat it out. 'What we're after, I take it, is to spread the game? You can count on old Neil. By the way, I've been thinking up a cheaper and easier leaf protein grinder and God – if there is such an entity – knows we have plenty of leaves after the wet. Storage would be no problem.'

'But would they like that?'

'I'd say so. My way. We'd get the leaves – properly. That could spread too. Bill Pirie would like that. I worked under him for a bit at Rothamsted. Oh, a long way back. We'd need to stop any big outfit grabbing it. No more PAX. Still and on, we've had our warning. Next time they won't get it out of us so easy.'

'It's possible' said Rahul uncertainly, 'that the Board is in a bit of trouble. It's being said that PAX is only a front for this Corporation, some kind of nasty monopoly. I don't know if it's true.'

'Of course it is!' said Neil, 'and the sooner we get rid of these buggers the sooner we get on with the job. On our own.'

He's confident, Rahul thought, but it may not work, any of it. We others are too deep in our complications and angers and worries and aggressions. And this grief that I've never had before, this grief that pains like an illness so that I can hardly bear it. Anne dead. No. Yes. But did I help to kill her? Not really. She wouldn't want me to think so even if it was true. Have we got to die for what we believe in? Perhaps none of us can be happy unless we have something to die for. But Anne just died of a heart attack. Like anyone. No, because it made her letter effective, made them ashamed not to take notice. But why so soon after I came back? If only I could have talked to her once more, there was so much I wanted to tell her, to hear from her, but she was dead when I heard my father shouting, when I ran into the room, lying there dead, not speaking to me, not looking –

But did Djiuvalji, did Neil, did at last Naburdja, pick up the pain out of his mind? How else were hands laid on him in kindness, so that he could think without anger, without bitterness, of Anne Tomlin whom he had pushed into writing that letter? And otherwise she might have rested, not driven her brave heart into fighting. She might be alive. And the Board not convinced. And where, where is Anne? Anne whom I love. Anne is now in and part of the Dreaming which is both then and forever now.